Tranquility Bight

a novella

If man is a piano key, the note he strikes
is sometimes out of tune.

Bahr Burr

HJB PRESS
Houston, TX

Tranquility Bight © 2023

First edition, December 2023

Published by HJB Press

 HJB PRESS

Houston, TX

Editing: Gail Fallen, gail@mesanetworks.net

Publishing and Design Services: Melinda Martin, melindamartin.me

ISBN: 979-8-9891777-0-7 (paperback); 979-8-9891777-1-4 (epub)

All glory to God, who created man not as a piano key to be played but as a being shaped in His image capable of voluntarily choosing what he most desires. Man's complete inability to incline his own heart toward righteousness neither lessens his guilt nor vindicates his evil intentions, but it sweetens the efficacious grace which willingly and irresistibly draws the undeserving elect from spiritual death to life through Christ's work on the cross (see Ephesians 2:1–10).

Contents

"[T]here are continually turning up in life moral and rational persons, sages and lovers of humanity who make it their object to live all their lives as morally and rationally as possible, to be, so to speak, a light to their neighbours simply in order to show them that it is possible to live morally and rationally in this world. And yet we all know that those very people sooner or later have been false to themselves, playing some queer trick, often a most unseemly one."

—Fyodor Dostoevsky
Notes from Underground

Deliberations

*Y*OU WOULD HAVE DONE THE SAME THING. THAT'S WHAT *I should've told him. That's what I did tell him, but he wouldn't listen. None of them did. Acted like they couldn't understand, wouldn't have done the same thing themselves. Think I'm different somehow. Especially evil or something. Keep telling yourselves that. Keep thinking you're somehow better than me or incapable of similar actions. That only bad people do that sort of thing. Now I'm one of the bad people. And they won't understand . . . he won't understand either . . . probably never will.*

But I'm getting ahead of myself. Thoughts been wandering a lot lately . . . mentioned it during her last visit. Could've been nicer about it, but I guess she's pretty stressed at the moment. Only natural. Kids are confused, she said. Don't understand why Daddy's gone. Why he doesn't come home. Still haven't been able to see them. Says it's not allowed, but I think she's lying. Can't bear them seeing their father like this. I understand, but it still pisses me off. Just seeing them once would be nice.

There, I did it again. Off on another tangent. Hard to focus right now with everyone around. Thought I'd get some privacy at this stage. Guess not. Can't be much longer. Everyone knows I did it . . . I told them. So now it's just the consequences. And I wait.

All the people, too . . . getting on my nerves. Wish friends and family wouldn't show up. Said it was to support me in my time of need. I don't need their damn support, especially if it means making me out as some sort of crazy person. Insanity defense? Sure. Whatever makes you feel better. But I'm not. And I meant to do it. And I knew it made no sense. But that's why I did it. Because making sense means nothing if you're just a pawn. And I'm not anyone's pawn. Make my own decisions. They'd do the same.

And that's what everyone needs to realize. I didn't make it clear enough. What did I say? I can't even remember at this point. Probably better that way. I'm sure I'll remember the end. The climax. The pronouncement of doom. Hope I can keep a straight face. He looks so ridiculous in that robe with that fat face of his bulging out behind those glasses. Like a cartoon character. He'll pronounce judgment, and I'll tell him to shove it. No. But I will tell him something. Something to wipe that condescending smirk off his face. What should I tell him?

You would have done the same thing!

Friday

THE SIGN LOOKED OLD, THE MAN THOUGHT. TOO OLD, given the type of neighborhood it represented. This was, after all, a pristine upper-middle-class community. Not ostentatiously wealthy but refined and modestly elegant. Not opulent so as to merit accusations of extravagance but exclusive enough to show that residents like himself were doing quite well in life.

But that sign spoiled everything. Anyone could derive an unfavorable impression of the neighborhood from its shabby appearance. The expensive houses, set back from the road and largely hidden from view, would be presumed equally shabby.

The sign looked dingy. A few older residents thought it rustic and claimed that its simple, rugged appearance gave the community a charmingly down-to-earth aspect. Real sturdy sign, that! Solid oak. Won't be blown down anytime soon. The man didn't care. The entrance to a respectable neighborhood was not the place for some well-intentioned retiree to display his amateur woodworking prowess for the whole world to observe and critique. Six years had passed, and the old geezer was long gone along with the other residents of the old township. He'd been the last to go, hanging on for a year after all the other old homes had been razed and replaced during the restoration. Now he was gone too, but his damn sign wasn't.

And then there was the name. TRANQUILITY BIGHT, the sign read. Not a bad name but somehow not quite right. Tranquility, at least, made sense, given the peaceful and serene nature of the community. But bight had something to do with the ocean, and the neighborhood was most certainly not by the ocean—or any body of water, for that matter. An hour's drive would change matters, but here one encountered mainly rolling hills and splendid greenery. The man now regretted voting in favor of the name along with everyone else.

Now, at long last, the sign would trouble him no longer. Last week's community mailer announced the pending installation of a new, modern sign to be installed shortly. The neighborhood governing panel, simply called the Board by most residents, had even stated the feature would include a tagline befitting their glorious community. From the man's perspective, it was about damn time.

❧

The man drove down the tree-lined avenue and into the neighborhood, quickly arriving at a large, two-story Mediterranean affair with a red roof and an immaculate white exterior. The kids were outside. He could tell by their playthings scattered over the yard and driveway and extending slightly into the thoroughfare.

Good it's a quiet street.

The kids shouted happily as the car approached. The playful ruckus made the man glad he'd gone to the expense of repaving the driveway the previous winter. Cobblestone looked attractive but made bouncing a ball or rollerblading difficult for young children. The smooth concrete driveway now facilitated outdoor play, a fact confirmed by the chalk drawings the man noticed as he pulled in.

"Daddy!"

"Daddy!"

"Hey, kiddos. Where's Mommy?"

"Inside. She watches through the window," the little girl said. "Can you play with us, Daddy?"

"Maybe in a few minutes, sweetie. Daddy has some work to do, and then Mommy might need him to help with dinner. It's Friday evening—do you know what that means?"

"Hot dogs!" the two children exclaimed simultaneously.

It was true—summer meant grilled franks on Friday nights if it didn't rain. It rarely rained. He usually grilled while his wife prepared the sides and dessert. This arrangement seemed to work well most of the time, except on those occasions when she made coleslaw.

Today won't be one of those days, though. Today is a good day.

Leaving work early had helped him miss the horrible traffic, giving him time to buy his wife some flowers as a surprise gift. He felt proud of himself for remembering that begonias were her favorite—she'd reminded him countless times during their decade of marriage, but he still usually managed to forget and buy her something else.

The man walked toward the house, admiring the neat, lush lawn. The hose trailed across the yard to the sprinkler. Most of his neighbors had automatic sprinkler systems, but he had kids. Kids liked to put on their bathing suits and run through the water, and that required an old-fashioned hose setup. The man smiled. He'd been a kid once, too.

The front door swung open as he approached. His wife stood in the entry for a brief moment before walking outside, shutting the door behind her.

She'll like the flowers.

She always did, but he could often detect her disappointment when he forgot and bought the wrong ones.

Not this time.

He looked at her and smiled, preparing a compliment to offer with the bouquet. She spoke first.

"The power's out. Been out for the last half hour. It's a good thing you were already planning on grilling—the stove and oven won't work."

Strange.

That sort of thing rarely happened. In fact, he couldn't remember it happening even once in this neighborhood. In new, modern communities such as theirs, things just didn't go wrong like they did elsewhere.

Not a big deal, though.

At least not enough to spoil the thought of a relaxing Friday evening, followed by a pleasant weekend.

His wife noticed the bouquet. She smiled.

"For me?"

"No, they're all mine." The man grinned.

"Let me put them in some water."

He handed her the bouquet and opened the door. Out of habit, he hit the light switch to illuminate the dim hallway—the switch was already on.

Right. Power's out.

It was still plenty light outside anyway. The long summer daylight hours would not fade into dusk until much later that evening.

The man deposited his briefcase on his home office desk and headed into the backyard. The kids enjoyed watching their father cook on the fancy gas grill and followed him outside for just that purpose.

Plenty left—that'll last several more meals.

The man set the propane tank down and soon had the hot dogs sizzling away. Within minutes, the kids were practically drooling as they watched him carefully remove each crispy brown frank and place them all in a heap on a plate.

"Food's ready," his wife called through the open back door.

He went inside to help her carry everything outdoors.

Please, no coleslaw.

Thankfully, tonight's side turned out to be a quinoa salad, a slightly preferable alternative. They carried the food and dishes outside, sat down in the lawn chairs, and began happily eating as a family.

"Can I have another?" the boy asked.

The man looked at his son and saw only a face covered in ketchup. His wife responded first.

"Eat some salad. And wipe your face."

The boy looked at his mother and grimaced. "I don't like it," he protested. "It has green slimy things."

"That's avocado—it's good for you."

"I don't like the little round things either. They don't taste like anything."

"The quinoa tastes like whatever else is in the salad. It's like rice—you like rice, don't you?"

"It doesn't taste like rice."

"You can either eat your salad, or I can give you some leftover cauliflower from the fridge. You want that instead?"

"No."

The girl finished her salad and served herself another frank.

The man finished his frank and paused to enjoy the perfect weather and a light breeze spreading the aroma of cooked food. He looked at the kids. They were growing too fast. The girl was almost seven and her brother two years younger. Born only yesterday, but here they were, going to school and scarfing hot dogs like seasoned veterans. The girl reached for her third. She could still outeat her brother, whose conscious efforts to outdo her sometimes had a negative effect on his gastrointestinal well-being.

"Daddy?"

The man snapped out of his reverie. "Yes, sweetie?"

"What are we doing this weekend?"

"Homework?"

"School's over, Daddy!" the girl said, laughing. "It finished two weeks ago."

"I know, sweetie—I'm just teasing. Why don't we go to the farmers' market? You want to get some sourdough cinnamon rolls tomorrow morning?"

"Yes!" the two children shouted together.

"Good! We'll do that in the morning and then Daddy will probably work in the yard a bit. Go wash up and choose a board game to play after dinner cleanup."

❧

The house had grown noticeably darker during the meal. The man threw dinner's trash in the garbage can.

We'll need a light source.

He had one, too. That battery-powered lantern used for camping last fall would do nicely. He rummaged in the hall closet for a few moments and eventually uttered a grunt of satisfaction as he withdrew the desired object from under a pink sleeping bag.

The doorbell rang. The man heard his wife open the door.

"Honey! Ryan wants to talk to you."

"What's up, Ryan?"

"Nothing much—happy Friday! Just checking to see if you knew what's going on with this power outage. I'd begun to think we were immune to this sort of thing."

"Don't know. I haven't been home too long, and we've been outside most of the time."

"Good day for it! Weather's just about perfect. I've been trying to get the family outside more, but the electronics always seem to win the popularity battle. I guess that's no longer an option, at least not until the power comes back on. Not that it will be much longer, I'd think."

The man nodded in agreement.

"You coming to the neighborhood social tomorrow?"

"Honestly, I completely forgot that's tomorrow, but yeah, I think we'll probably go. We have morning plans, but our afternoon and evening should be open."

"Glad to hear—everyone I've talked to will be going. You don't go that often yourself. Anyone you don't like to be around?"

"I get along with most people in general," the man replied. "I've just been busy. The family usually goes without me."

"Well, as long as you're there tomorrow, it doesn't matter." Ryan reflected for a moment. "If all neighborhoods had social events and got to know each other, the world would be a better place. All communities should be like ours. We're a model for social interaction if ever I've seen one."

The man agreed but did not want to encourage further dialogue. His next-door neighbor could talk endlessly at times. He was usually right in what he said, but he took a while to say it.

Ryan's smartphone buzzed. "It's the wife—gotta go help with the kiddos. I'll see you tomorrow evening."

"Sounds good."

As the front door closed, the two children came tramping into the living room carrying the board game of choice.

Friday nights are hard to beat.

Saturday

THE PREVIOUS EVENING HAD NOT GONE WELL. AFTER A pleasant dinner and the family game, the full implications of the power outage became evident, the lack of light being the most pressing issue. It all started enjoyably enough, the family gathered around the table with the lantern casting a glow over the board and playing pieces. It was like camping, but indoors. The novelty soon wore off, however, especially when the kids went upstairs to get in their pajamas and brush their teeth. The lack of light was scary, they said. The man gave the one flashlight he'd found to the girl and then followed the boy around holding the lantern.

The boy woke up around 1 a.m. to go to the bathroom. Needing a light, he tiptoed into the master bedroom, only to knock over a cheap vase with a crash, waking the man from his fitful sleep. Shortly after returning to bed, the man heard the distant humming of a motor start in the blackness outside. Started . . . and never stopped.

Probably a generator of some sort. Great.

He tried to think of it as a substitute for his white noise machine, but a combustion engine lacked the soothing effect of ocean waves or a rippling brook.

He eventually fell asleep again, only to be awakened by the girl asking, "When can we get our cinnamon rolls, Daddy?" The man grunted in frustration and looked at the clock. He'd overslept. So had his wife.

As they prepared to leave, the man inspected the entire house. Briefly opening the refrigerator door, he checked the temperature.

Still got some time left. Not much, though.

Getting out the door took forever. The kids were hungry and grumpy, and the man's wife managed to take a full half hour to brush her teeth and hair. Right before leaving, the boy poured himself a glass of orange juice while leaving the fridge door open, allowing precious cold air to escape.

The trip to the farmers' market briefly restored order while the children contentedly covered their faces with cream cheese frosting, only to become unmanageable bundles of energy by the time the family arrived home.

"Go play, children," their mother said firmly. "You need to burn off that sugar."

The kids began rollerblading up and down the driveway, leaving the man and his wife inside. While not exactly hot, the house did feel stuffy. The man opened a few windows and immediately felt better.

The afternoon passed uneventfully, the man trying to enjoy a nap while his wife attended one of her club meetings.

Generator's still running.

He slipped into a doze.

❧

They arrived at the neighborhood social around seven, the man feeling rested and the kids happy and hungry from their afternoon of playing. The man noticed the high turnout as they approached the clubhouse. The smell of food wafted past his nose as he spied Ryan at the patio by one of the large propane grills, wearing an apron and animatedly conversing with several people.

"So, you did come! Brought the whole family, too!"

"Yup, we're here. Nice apron, by the way. Really suits your figure."

"Hilarious. What'll you have?"

"What's cooking?"

"We've got beef patties, hot dogs, veggie burgers, and fish filets all ready to go."

The family was soon munching away on their personal favorites. As he ate, the man scanned the crowd for familiar faces. He recognized several, mainly belonging to neighbors he'd seen before but never officially met. As kids played, adults crowded around the patio and its supply of food or congregated in small groups around the large grassy lawn. Ice chests and coolers littered the patio.

At least the power outage won't affect that stuff. Unlike my food at home.

Plenty of daylight remained, but the man could see portable lights already set up. He thought about flashlights and the fact he'd forgotten to buy some on the way home that morning.

I'll do it tomorrow.

He noticed Ryan—now without his apron—talking to some close neighbors, hands moving almost as fast as his mouth. The man approached the little group.

Raymond Stickler, his neighbor directly across the street, stood listening to Ryan, along with a disinterested-looking Blake and Mandy Goins, Ryan's next-door neighbors. A few other residents, including stuffy Ms. Perkins, the rich spinster from down the street, completed the small group. Everyone but Ryan acknowledged the man's arrival with a look or a nod. Ryan continued speaking.

"I don't know why the power's been out, but I bet that Bates fellow is at the bottom of it. I haven't seen him here; otherwise, I'd ask him about it straight out. He knows what's going on—I'm sure of it! Might even be responsible himself."

"How could he be responsible?" Raymond queried.

"Easy! Bates controls everything in this neighborhood. Everyone knows he owns a bunch of the houses, but not everyone's aware of the fact his investment firm owns the utility company that keeps the lights on around here."

"I'm not sure that's correct," Raymond retorted. "Besides, having stake in a company wouldn't be the same as controlling actual operations. You almost made it sound like he created the outage on purpose!"

"It did sound that way, didn't it?"

The man didn't like Ryan's smirk or the direction the conversation was heading. Ms. Perkins looked ready to launch into one of her moralistic tirades—perhaps on the nature of public utilities—and he tried to head her off.

"How's it going, Raymond? Blake, Mandy—how are you both?"

Raymond gave him a distracted nod. The Goins couple looked visibly relieved at being released from their part in a one-sided conversation. Blake then spoke.

"Doing good, considering. Honestly, I have no experience with this sort of thing, and Mandy is struggling with her work-from-home job, too. Any word on when the power comes back on? Heard any rumors?"

"Nope, not me," the man responded lightly, still trying to steer the conversation in a different direction. "Got any plans for tomorrow?"

"No, I'll probably just live at the library or maybe a coffee shop for a while. Not much else to do, really."

"Seems like a perfect time to think of others for once, Mr. Goins," Ms. Perkins interjected haughtily. "I'll be spending my Sunday morning helping those in need. My charity club is distributing flower bouquets to the homeless in the Big City. It never hurts to bring a little beauty into the lives of the unfortunate among us—they need beauty as much as we do."

"How will flowers help people living in tents?" Ryan blurted out, realizing too late the harsh nature of his comment. Ms. Perkins glared at him.

"As for you, Mr. Jackson, I can't recall having ever seen you help the needy. Where's your heart toward your fellow man?"

"I help out plenty!" Ryan protested. "Becky and I just made a considerable donation to—"

"No matter, it's not my place to judge. I just believe in the goodness of my fellow man and want everyone to have a chance in life. Do you believe in the goodness of man, Mr. Stickler?"

Raymond, clearly taken by surprise, looked confused. "Uh . . . well, sure. Who doesn't?"

"So do we," interjected Blake, preemptively deflecting the query headed his way. "Man's good at heart—just needs to be trusted."

The man felt the hawk-like expression before Ms. Perkins had even turned toward him. "And you, sir?"

"I think people are basically good," he began. "Of course, nobody's perfect, but most people just want a chance to succeed in life. There are a few bad apples, but they're not like the rest of us."

"What about you, Mr. Bracken?" Nobody had noticed the figure standing just outside the small circle, listening quietly.

"Do I believe humans are basically good, you mean?"

"Yes, that's what I mean."

"Are you referring to the acts that humans commit or their capacity to commit those acts?"

"What difference does that make?" Ms. Perkins huffed impatiently. "Are humans good or not?"

"It makes a significant difference. If we're talking about the acts humans commit, then I'd agree that most people act in a relatively good manner in the general sense of the word. If, however, we're talking about the human capacity to commit evil, then I'd say no one is truly good."

"No one?" replied Ms. Perkins, shocked.

"No one."

"But what about all the goodness around us?" the spinster protested. "Are you seriously saying nobody does good?"

"No, that's exactly what I'm *not* saying. People do good—we see it all the time. I'm simply pointing out that each and every individual has the innate capacity to do evil. Most don't, but that's due more to the lack of motivation or a fear of consequences than any real morality."

"Well, I never! Most people are good, and only terrible people can do terrible things!"

"I disagree."

"Who asked for your opinion?"

"You did, actually. It seemed a strange topic for a neighborhood gathering, but I'm happy to oblige and share my viewpoint."

"I wish you hadn't! I've lived five decades on this earth and never heard anything more ridiculous! Am I not right?" she asked, addressing the others.

Everyone remained awkwardly silent, caught between Ms. Perkin's overbearing attitude and Bracken's disturbing comments. Mike Bracken and his family had always been a bit different from the other residents. They'd moved in a few houses down from Raymond about six months ago; the new household, despite making attempts to interact with their neighbors, just didn't seem to fit in. The man had never spoken more than a few words to Bracken and now felt himself even less inclined to pursue any sort of relationship. He made a final valiant effort to change the subject of the conversation.

"Blake, you up for tennis tomorrow? I thought—"

A general murmur among the crowd cut him short. Ryan spoke.

"The top dog's arrived."

❧

A large Mercedes with a custom paint job pulled into one of the reserved spots directly in front of the clubhouse. Out stepped a man around fifty years of age, sporting flip-flops, beach shorts, and an expensive Hawaiian shirt. His slicked hair glistened with a cosmetic sheen, and his sunglasses seemed out of place in the fading evening light. After pausing by his car long enough to draw everyone's attention, he sauntered toward the pavilion with easy, confident strides.

Ryan turned and whispered to the group. "Mr. Big has entered the building. You think I should ask him about my theory?"

"What theory?" Raymond questioned, already forgetting the previous conversation. The man remembered, though, and feared a flare-up of Bates's infamous temper.

"No, Ryan, don't bring it up. It's ridiculous anyway. Why don't you ask him where he got that shirt instead? You could do with some summer style yourself."

Ryan ignored the jibe and stepped a few paces forward to greet the approaching tycoon.

"Bates! What's new in your world? Making money and living large, I presume?"

"You said it—Riley, is it?"

"Ryan," came the cheerful response. "25552 Ocean Breeze Drive. Two-story stucco with the red tile roof and palms out front. One of the few properties around here you don't own yourself."

"Oh, it's not as many as that," Bates replied modestly. "Most of my neighbors don't owe me a cent or depend on me in any way whatsoever."

"Except for their utilities, you mean," Ryan prompted.

"Utilities?"

"You know—electricity, running water, and so on. From what I've heard, you're quite the utilities magnate. I bet you could end this outage with the flick of a switch, huh?"

"I wish I could," Bates replied, scanning the crowd and cracking his knuckles. "I can't change the power situation, if that's what you're talking about."

"Yup, that's what I mean. You own the power company, right?"

"No—I've got business dealings with 'em, but I don't own it. Could, though, if I wanted to. Why all the questions, Riley?"

"Oh, you know, just trying to work out whether we could bribe you to fix this whole power situation for us."

"Forget it. Believe me, it's unpleasant for me too."

"Not as unpleasant as it is for those around you, Mr. Bates," interjected Ms. Perkins. "Besides, even if I had your financial means, I wouldn't change a thing! It does one good to be uncomfortable once in a while. I doubt living in a mansion with your every need provided for can really be called unpleasant."

Bates smirked and surveyed the crowd. He wanted public admiration, not a harangue from a self-righteous harridan.

Turning on his heels without even so much as a goodbye, he sauntered over to a larger group of residents.

Ryan faced his friends. "Not very forthcoming, was he?"

"Actually, he was quite forthcoming—he pretty much destroyed your theory," the man responded. "Anyone up for coffee and donuts tomorrow morning?"

He immediately regretted asking everyone, but thankfully, only Ryan, Blake, and Raymond accepted. Ms. Perkins merely sniffed contemptuously and trundled off. Mike Bracken declined. The man looked around.

House will be dark soon.

"I've got to take the kids home," he said.

❧

The kids had to be dragged all the way home, the boy angrily shouting that his sister had gotten a snow cone but he hadn't. It took a full hour to get both children to bed. They complained about the darkness and the heat. The man berated them but secretly shared their concerns. The heat was becoming oppressive.

After dealing with the children, the man and his wife went straight to bed, where she fell asleep immediately, but he lay awake, listening to the generator.

He checked his phone battery level around midnight to ensure his alarm would work.

Twenty percent. Must charge it at the coffee shop in the morning.

Sunday

THE MAN ROLLED OUT OF BED AT SEVEN, FULL OF BLEARY-eyed regret for making a morning appointment. The house felt calm but stifling. He considered opening the windows, but decided against it, fearing insects indoors. He grimaced. His wife had urged him countless times to buy window screens, but he'd never gotten around to it.

She'll say, "I told you so!!"

He checked the fridge. A weak gust of cool air hit his face as he opened the door. The milk jugs dripped with condensation.

Damn it—it's all going to spoil.

He sat down at the kitchen table and tried to remember the day's tasks.

Flashlights.

He rubbed his eyes groggily.

Sundays shouldn't be like this.

Sleep provided rest and blissful ignorance of his problems.

He heard a door close upstairs and immediately stood up. One of the kids was awake. Grabbing his loafers, he stealthily made his way outside. If he was up early, his wife should be as well. She could handle the kids.

The sun shone brightly.

Summer's almost here.

The man glanced at Ryan's empty driveway.

Must've left already.

"Good morning!"

The man turned around. A young man in his late twenties waved at him from the next driveway. He was dressed in compression shorts and a tight-fitting racing bib and held a cycling helmet in one hand.

"Morning, Kurt. Off on a ride?"

"Yup—good day for it, too! Can't let my routine get disrupted, even if everyone is freaked out about the power outage. Take care!" He rode off, pedaling vigorously.

The man yawned and watched him go. He barely knew Kurt, but his neighbor seemed pleasant enough.

Another sound drew his attention. Further down the street, Mike Bracken was opening the door of a Chevy Tahoe parked in his driveway. Two young kids trooped out the front door, followed by Mrs. Bracken, carrying a young infant.

The man watched them load up into the SUV.

Up early, all of them. And wearing matching outfits.

Bracken noticed him and waved. The man nodded in return, trying not to dwell on the contrast between the family's coordinated wardrobe and his own rumpled appearance.

A thought struck him. He hopped in his car and rolled down the street, lowering the window as he approached Bracken's now-deserted house.

So that's where the generator is.

He couldn't see it, but, by the sound, he could tell it must be on Bracken's property. It all made sense now—the Bracken family had power.

No wonder they look so put together.

The thought annoyed him.

He reached the neighborhood entrance and stopped, trying to remember his intended destination.

Right, coffee shop.

He grimaced as he glanced at his watch, then rolled the windows down and hit the accelerator.

☙

The coffee and donuts improved his mood. His neighbors also looked fatigued and did not begrudge his tardy arrival. They discussed the power outage, the man mentioning Bracken's generator. The others had all noticed the sound but did not seem particularly bothered by the noise. What did trouble them, Ryan especially, was the lack of community spirit use of such resources showed.

"We're all in this together—if one suffers, we should show solidarity by sharing the pain," Ryan said.

The man sped toward the Big City, running through his mental checklist of tasks to accomplish. He knew he'd probably forget something and frustrate his wife, but he could never bring himself to write things down.

☙

Returning home in time for a late lunch, he found the kids running rampant indoors even though it felt nicer outside.

Much nicer. A wave of hot, dusty air hit him as he walked through the front door. He sneezed.

He found his wife in the kitchen, putting a host of food items on the floor in front of an open refrigerator.

"What are you doing? We need to keep the door closed so the food doesn't spoil."

"Already has," she replied sullenly. "Some of it, anyway. I hope you brought some nonperishables back with you."

I knew I'd forget something.

"You sure it's spoiled? I've been checking on a regular basis."

"Of course I'm sure! Feel this milk carton—it's barely even cold. Most of the stuff in here is worthless at this point. The freezer is still pretty cold, but it's almost empty. Why didn't you transfer items to the freezer? They would have kept longer."

"I didn't know the outage would last this long. I've been focused on other issues. What have you been doing besides complaining?"

She glanced at him sharply. "I've been cleaning."

"Hence the dust storm. Couldn't you have waited until we can get some air moving through here? And why are the kids inside? They should take that ruckus outdoors."

"I'm doing the best I can! I got too busy with the house-work to pay much attention, and they were playing peacefully until just a few minutes ago. Something must have happened to excite them."

She was right. The discovery of a moth in an upstairs closet had resulted in a house-wide, no-holds-barred chase, the moth the sought-after prize. The children had, just the moment before, attained said prize by squashing the unfortunate lepidopteran into a smear on the living room wall.

He sent the kids outside and lent his grudging support to the fridge cleaning project. This effort yielded some not-so-frozen vegetables and chicken nuggets as the sum total of their unspoiled perishables.

The man looked in the pantry. Cereal, rice, canned beans, tomato sauce. Sardines, cookies, roasted peanuts, random packaged pastries. Canned chicken soup and a bag of millet flour from a previous century. The prospects looked dull indeed.

"Let's get takeout tonight," he told his wife.

დ

The windows were open. The bugs would come in, but so would the light breeze. The lantern sat on the kitchen table, surrounded by styrofoam boxes from the Asian takeout the family had ravenously devoured. Leaning back in his chair, the man let out a grunt of satisfaction. He wanted to relax before dealing with the difficult task of getting the kids to bed.

At least they both have their own flashlights now.

A soft tapping sound interrupted his mental reverie. Barely audible, it seemed to come from the front hallway. He grabbed the lantern and went to investigate, inadvertently leaving the occupied table in darkness. Entering the hallway, he recognized the sound as a light rapping on the front door.

Who could be coming over this late?

He opened the door and peered at the dark form standing a few feet away. Raising the lantern, he scrutinized the figure before him.

The light revealed a short, frail-looking man wearing spectacles. Flecks of black tinged his short gray beard and hair. He nervously shifted his weight from one foot to another, a bowler hat clasped in his hands. Dressed in trousers and tweed vest and sporting a bowtie, he appeared a character from a bygone era. The man recognized the old professor.

An aura of mystery surrounded the professor. Few saw him, fewer spoke to him, and many residents had never even laid eyes on him. Those who had spoken to him always remembered his soft, wavering voice and strange accent. He purportedly hailed from some distant country in Central Asia. "One of the 'stans," Ryan had once conjectured.

He lived in the most remote part of the neighborhood, in a secluded yet elegant house at the end of the last street. No one had seen him move in—he was just there. No one knew why he was called the professor—he just *was*.

He had strange habits. Those who lived closest sometimes noticed an ancient station wagon leaving the house when normal people were still asleep. It seemed odd—such a car did not match such a house. Days would go by without the vehicle leaving the driveway, and then it would be gone for a week. He seemed averse to light, as none ever shone through the curtains. He routinely received shipments of large crates full of ancient-looking books. He lived alone, apart from an elderly housekeeper. The property and house reflected meticulous upkeep. Although considered eccentric by his neighbors, the studious little man with the funny accent engendered more curiosity than outright dislike.

This unique individual now stood on the man's doorstep. The man had never spoken to the professor, his only interaction being a recent attempt to return a book he'd found, a massive old tome written in a strange language. The man had placed it by the professor's front door, hoping he had guessed correctly as to its owner. That was a month ago now.

"It hot inside, eh?"

The man shook himself. "Sorry?"

"It hot inside, no?"

"Yeah, uh, pretty hot. No air conditioning—gets hot without air conditioning," he said slowly, enunciating every syllable. He immediately felt stupid.

"I know this," the professor said, the slight hint of a smile on his face. "I take precautions to make sure my house stay cold all the time."

Precautions. That's a substantial word. Maybe he speaks better than the accent would indicate.

"Yeah, that's a good idea," the man responded lamely. "I wish we'd done the same. But the power will come back on soon."

The professor stood silently, his spectacles giving his large, unblinking eyes an owl-like appearance. It was an odd face.

The Face.

"Can I help you with something?" The man hated the formal tone, but he didn't know what else to say. Besides, the Face with its owl eyes made him uncomfortable.

"You already did," the professor replied.

"I did? When?"

"Some time ago. You give me something I value much. It very magnanimous of you."

Magnanimous?

The man coughed uncertainly. "I'm afraid I don't understand."

"My book—you return my book to me, no?"

The man remembered. "Oh yes, that was me. I wasn't even sure it was your book. I found it at the nature station one Saturday morning and figured it might be yours, especially with the strange writing and all."

"It is mine, and it very important to me. Very old, unique specimen. I sometime go to listen to the night at late hour when nobody disturb me. I bring book but left it like a fool!" He slapped his forehead in frustration. "You read the classics?"

"Classics?"

"Tolstoy, Dostoevsky . . . the classics."

"Uh . . . yeah, sure."

"You like them, no?"

"I, uh . . ."

"They are all work of genius. I read them many time. This one you return to me is perhaps my most favorite."

"What is it?"

"In your language, it is called *War and Peace*."

"That's *War and Peace*? And you've read the whole thing?"

"Seven time. I read it again now."

"But why? Isn't there something else you can read?"

"Plenty, but I always come back to this book. This very special copy. If it rain before you find, I lose forever."

"Well, I'm glad I could help," the man responded restlessly. Thankfully, the professor looked ready to leave.

"I go now," he said. "Many thanks for your punctilious aid."

"Okay, bye." The man closed the door.

"Punctilious?" he muttered aloud.

☙

"It means diligent or attentive to detail," his wife said. "It's not used that often, but it's a good word to know. I'm just surprised he knew it. He seems nice enough, though."

"Yeah."

"I didn't know you returned his book. Did you look at it before you brought it back? If it's as curious as its owner, it must be quite interesting."

"I couldn't read it, remember? It was in Russian or something and extremely fragile."

"It's good you found it. The professor didn't strike me as the nature type. What did he say—listen to the night? I wonder what that means. Never thought he'd just show up here like that."

"Me neither."

"Can you put the lantern back on the table?"

"Yeah, okay. Guess I better clean up all this trash."

A thought struck him. "What happened to the kids? Weren't they here before the professor came over?"

"They finished eating. I guess they've overcome their fear of the dark enough to venture to some other part of the house."

She was right. The kids had trooped off and were found in an upstairs hallway, facing each other and taking turns counting the number of seconds each could withstand gazing directly into the other's flashlight. At the moment the man approached, the boy had just finished an attempt of an ill-advised length that left him teary-eyed and temporarily blind.

Getting them ready for bed took ages. The man managed to perform the necessary rituals while raising his voice only a few times. He trudged back down the stairs holding his flashlight, exhausted and ready for sleep.

Tomorrow's Monday.

The thought wasn't pleasant.

Monday

THE MAN'S PHONE BUZZED. PUTTING HIS SANDWICH DOWN, he grabbed his phone and noticed a chain of text messages from his wife, all of which conveyed a sense of deep frustration and annoyance.

The kids were desperate for things to do, summer activities still not starting for a couple weeks. She couldn't wash clothes. It was hot. She had allergies. She had to eat her canned soup cold. Bugs and generator noise came in through the open windows. Et cetera, et cetera.

The man shoved the phone into his briefcase and continued his lunch. He had his own problems. Besides, things weren't really that bad. The power situation was inconvenient, not catastrophic. He could buy whatever they needed. At least he wasn't homeless like that guy he'd seen on his way to work.

The man complimented himself on this new positive mindset but left the buzzing phone in his briefcase.

❧

The drive home was brutal. Traffic seemed even worse than normal. On the way home, he bought several boxes of frozen shish kabobs and some ice cream sandwiches. His wife left for her event without speaking to him, clearly not appreciating the unanswered text messages from earlier in the day. The man, engaged in checking his voicemail, gave absent-minded consent to the children's request to eat the dessert they'd already found, and by the time he went outside to get the grill going, both children had messy faces and sticky hands.

The bright sunset and light breeze felt refreshing after the stifling indoors. The man opened the shish kabobs only to realize he'd bought the shrimp variety.

Damn it.

He disliked shrimp, and the kids avoided it like the plague.

Maybe they'll try it if it's grilled. And they'll like the pineapple.

He started the grill.

"What's on the menu?"

The man turned. Kurt stood on his pool deck watching over the short fence.

"Shish kabobs. You want some? I got the wrong kind by mistake."

"Nah, I'm good. Good idea, though—I've got some tilapia my buddy gave me that's been sitting in the freezer. I've been meaning to drag the grill out and get her going since early spring. It needs cleaning and maybe a few other things."

The man didn't respond. The first whiffs of the sizzling shrimp had hit him with disturbing intensity. He looked up at Kurt.

"Well, let me know if you change your mind."

Kurt headed inside without further comment.

The kids didn't like the kabobs. They picked off the pineapple and then requested another ice cream sandwich apiece.

"You can have another one if you promise to be good about bedtime tonight."

"We promise, Daddy."

After dinner, the man cleaned up and sat down to relax just as the doorbell rang. Telling the kids to grab their flashlights and get ready for bed, he opened the door.

"You read the news?" Ryan asked.

"What news?"

"On the community bulletin page."

"Page? Where?"

"Um, hello—the internet!" Ryan laughed. "I should've known you don't keep up with the neighborhood news."

"No, not really. Mostly I get it from neighbors if it's important."

And sometimes even if it isn't.

"Well, anyway, the Board has called a meeting for tomorrow night. They say everyone needs to be there to discuss the power situation and its impact on the community."

"Right now, I mainly just care about its impact on me. Tuesday nights aren't great—we're generally pretty busy."

"They're pretty adamant about it. I think it's a good idea, especially since we have to tackle this problem as a group."

"I'd like to tackle whoever's responsible for the outage," the man replied. "It's getting annoying. We'll probably just end up talking a bunch and not making any decisions."

"Don't be so pessimistic. We'll get it solved if we all band together."

The man saw his wife's car pull in the driveway, the headlights bright in the strangely dark streets. His wife noticed the front door open.

"Hi, Ryan."

"Hullo! I'm just telling your husband about the meeting tomorrow." He promptly informed her of the upcoming event.

"I think that's a good idea," she responded. "Get everyone involved and sharing the burden together."

The man remained silent, and Ryan noticed.

"He doesn't want to go."

The man felt his wife's critical gaze. She was just about to speak when several loud thumping noises came from upstairs.

"The kids aren't in bed?"

"I told them to get ready for bed—they promised earlier they'd be good about bedtime."

"They promised? I hope you didn't give them anything as a bribe. How did dinner go?"

"Fine," the man responded cryptically.

"Well, I guess I'll have to finish the job you started," she huffed. "Excuse me, gentlemen."

Ryan resumed the conversation. "The meeting's not really optional. I mean, it is, but it isn't. The Board requires attendance from at least one adult member of each household. They can make your life difficult if you don't go."

"I know all that," the man responded gloomily. "I'm going, but I'm not happy about it."

"Clearly!" Ryan said with a laugh. "I'm glad you're going. I was once on the receiving end of the Board's attention and it wasn't a pleasant experience. Still, they're a necessary evil of sorts. I just wish they'd apply the rules evenly."

"Meaning what, exactly?"

"Well, they didn't want me doing maintenance on my convertible in the driveway, but when someone like the professor drives a beater all the time, that's totally acceptable."

"He came over here."

"Who did?"

"The professor."

"To your house? When?" Ryan asked incredulously.

"Last night. He wanted to thank me for returning a book I'd found."

"I'll be danged! The old man does venture out after all! Maybe he'll show up tomorrow, then. I've heard rumors he's more prepared than most for this crisis."

"He did say something about keeping his house cold."

"That sounds amazing right now," Ryan said, turning away. "Catch you later!"

The man closed the door.

Tuesday

"THIS MEETING IS CALLED TO ORDER. EVERYONE, PLEASE make sure you've signed in. Please quiet down, folks—we're about to get started."

The speaker, Lawrence Fisher, was a short, plump man with an ostentatious manner. He smiled at the residents up front paying close attention and scowled at those who had brought their kids. As chairman of the Board, he feared disruptions and felt he was far too important a man to be repeating himself.

The room gradually quieted as Fisher waited. He wanted the entire community focused on him before speaking. He cast a final stern glance around the room, his demeanor expressing somber responsibility. All was quiet.

"As you know, this meeting was called in response to the unusual, inconvenient, and preposterous conditions the residents of this neighborhood now face as a result of the power outage. It is the opinion of the Board and myself that this outage is patently absurd and simply unacceptable for an upstanding, tax-paying, unique, and vibrant community such as ours. We mean to get to the bottom of it, I promise you that!"

Fisher started pacing back and forth across the stage.

"Yes, I promise you that," he repeated. "We will get to the bottom of this outrage. The people of this community should not be preoccupied with such issues. We should be changing the world, not the water in our toilets!"

A few sympathetic snickers.

"We should be lighting society with bright ideas, not lighting our hallways with flashlights!"

Heads nodding.

"We should have heated ovens, not overheated children!"

A general murmur of approval swept through the gathered assembly.

"Personally, I can withstand many hardships, as can many of you. I am always encouraged to see such resilience—it gives me a deep sense of pride in our shared community. This isn't about us, mind you, but rather our children, the elderly, and all those who suffer most. Friends, this situation, while uncomfortable for us, is becoming intolerable for them and must be resolved for their sake.

"We all lead busy lives, I know. I realize many of you were upset about having to show up tonight. Let me assure you, it is quite necessary. The needs of the community can only be met by the community as a whole. The Board has already gone to great lengths to make sure this community hall is fully operational with lighting and air conditioning so we can meet comfortably. So sit back, folks, and enjoy yourselves tonight as we conduct important work."

Fisher paused. He felt pleased with the way things were going.

"Let's get down to business, shall we? The first item will be an update about the power outage itself, followed by a discussion of the known issues facing the community and its residents. The meeting will close with general proposals and any decisions the Board deems it necessary and proper to make."

A hand went up in the audience.

"Please hold questions until later, thank you. We'll take care of everyone. Now it's time for the first order of business—please welcome Mr. Desmond Skates, the Board's current director of community resources and utility management."

A thin, bookish-looking man rose from a long table onstage and moved toward the chairman, leaving several others still sitting quietly.

Probably Board members.

He took the microphone.

"Good evening, everyone," he began in a thin, quavering voice that made him sound perpetually nervous. "As director of community resources and utility management, it is my responsibility to share all the information the Board has obtained concerning the current power outage. At this time, despite earnest efforts and continued investigation, the root cause of the outage has not yet been discovered."

A subdued murmur of exasperation swept through the hall. Skates glanced around uneasily but continued.

"Let me assure everyone we are working night and day to get to the bottom of this. The lack of precedent for this type of situation has left many in our community uncertain as to the future. We are working to ensure this is both the first and the last time we experience such events.

"Let's not forget the numerous benefits of living in a small community such as ours. As you all know, Tranquility Bight is a neighborhood but also its own micro municipality. We have our own police and fire service, pay separate taxes, and address our mail differently. Most of the time, the services for which we pay a premium are vastly superior in quality and reliability to those provided to residents of the Big City. I assure you, this sort of thing happens to them all the time. We are not currently aware of any other outages in the greater area. Information is hard to come by but will be passed along as soon as we receive it.

"One final note. Please leave the handling of everything to the Board. This situation requires delicacy and a measured use of bargaining power, both of which the Board can display to a much greater extent than any individual resident. Thank you for your understanding."

The chairman recovered the microphone as the crowd sat in disappointed silence.

"Thank you, Desmond. As you can see, folks, we're doing all we can to solve this problem. The next item on the agenda is a discussion of current issues. For that, please welcome the Board's Community Outreach Coordinator, Ms. Amber Richmond."

A tall, middle-aged woman with short dark hair addressed the audience.

"Good evening, everyone. I hope most of you know me by now—community interaction is my job, after all. The past few days, I've had discussions with many residents, both in person and on our social media pages, and I now have a pretty good idea of the current issues faced by members of our community. The stories I've heard from you all have reminded me of the responsibility we have as a community to come together and help each other as much as possible. I'm going to keep my message short for the sake of time, but I want everyone to know that the Board recognizes the difficulty of this situation and wants to take a personalized approach wherever possible in providing assistance. We will address specific needs later, but, for now, please continue using our social media groups to communicate your requests. Finally, please remember our resources are limited and we are doing our best to help each and every household. Thank you."

Fisher took the microphone.

"Thank you, Ms. Richmond. Folks, as she said, please make sure to take full advantage of the online resources available to you. And now, let us turn to the final and most involved stage of this meeting. First, I will share some updates approved by the Board. Following these short remarks, I will moderate an open discussion so residents have the opportunity to ask specific questions.

"Right, decisions. First, the Board has decided to postpone any and all community activities scheduled for this upcoming week, including the seasonal opening of the pool facilities. Second, the Board is working to make sure this meeting hall remains operational during the power outage. Third, please limit any requests for assistance to items related to the outage. Less pressing issues can wait. Fourth and finally, the Board reserves the right to call additional meetings later this week should the need arise.

"Thanks for your patience, folks. I'd now like to switch gears and start a community dialogue. So, without further ado, let's get started."

∾

The man listened with a growing sense of disappointment and frustration. As far as he could tell, nobody actually seemed to know anything.

Talk is cheap—what's the point of the Board if they don't actually do anything?

He remained silent, however.

"Thanks for waiting, everyone," Fisher began. "Now's the fun part—the time where you all get to interact. First, we'll open the floor for questions, and then we'll provide a chance for people to offer suggestions and raise any important issues we've missed. We've got a half hour left, so if you've got a question, raise your hand, and a volunteer will get you a microphone."

No one in the audience moved.

"Come on, don't be shy, folks!" the chairman encouraged in his most jovial manner. "We can't answer questions that aren't asked. And by the way, there's no such thing as a stupid question."

One hand went up. "Is our community the only one affected?"

Fisher frowned as he reconsidered his last statement. "I believe Mr. Skates already addressed that subject. Anything to add, Desmond?"

"We are unaware of any other outages at this time," Skates responded flatly.

"Questions . . .?" Fisher scanned the crowd. A middle-aged man sitting with his wife near the back stood up.

"Are there any community regulations concerning individual measures one may take to restore power? Batteries, generators, that sort of thing?"

Fisher looked at Skates. "Utilities is your area of expertise, Desmond."

"True, but this is more a compliance issue," Skates said, deferring. "Tim, anything we should know here?"

One of the figures at the table glanced up.

"Uh, not really," he responded. "By the way, everyone, I'm Tim Barlette, your community regulations compliance manager. I make sure community guidelines and policies are understood and observed. I act on behalf of our Homeowners' Association, which reports directly to the Board and works to keep this community safe and beautiful for all its residents.

"As to your question, the community does not have restrictions on the use of external power sources as such.

Safety, of course, is paramount, and we reserve the right to intervene should any resident act in a manner that places his or her neighbors in danger."

Fisher pointed to a young woman with one hand raised and a squirming child in the other arm. "Please go ahead, ma'am."

"My name is Emily Troubet. My husband and I have lived here for five months now, and we like the safe atmosphere it provides for our kids. My question is whether there will be some sort of support network arranged for those who are most in need of assistance? We talk about helping the community as a whole, but it might be necessary to focus on specific families that need help the most."

"Absolutely," Fisher interjected. "We do care about individuals. That said, a community is many people, and the needs of that group naturally deserve more focus than the needs of a few individuals. I expect this entire situation to be resolved shortly, but, in the meantime, we will try to make decisions that benefit as many people as possible."

Fisher pointed to another woman in the audience. "Ms. Galway?"

"Yes, thank you, I've been waiting my turn patiently, but I guess no one noticed since I don't have kids making a bunch of noise." She glared at Emily Troubet, who blushed and sat down. "No matter, no matter. My husband and I"—she pointed to a timid-looking man huddled in the chair beside her—"believe this crisis calls for a measure of resource distribution not currently in place. I've noticed that some residents are more able to deal with this crisis than others. Some have more supplies, and a few even have electricity in their homes through various preparations, the likes of which not all community members have the expertise to employ. I have empathy for everyone in my community and don't want anyone to suffer. Would it be possible for the Board to implement some sort of initiative forcing . . . enabling those most prepared to assist those who are struggling? This could take the form of material resources or cognitive expertise, thus ensuring all residents share in any solutions implemented."

"Yes, absolutely," Fisher responded cheerily. "We have a diverse community full of interesting and skilled people willing to lend their fellow man a hand. I don't doubt—"

"That's not what I meant," Rose Galway quickly interjected. "It's all well and fine to have people help out when it's convenient. I'm talking about a system that centralizes the sharing of knowledge and physical labor."

"Yes, I understand, Ms. Galway, and I'm sure many people have extra resources they'd be willing to share. In fact, my wife and I—"

"I'm not talking about being willing to share. I'm talking about a general sharing of resources regardless of how people feel about it. That's the only way to make sure the neediest are cared for."

"Yes, and any supplies the Board can obtain for the community will be shared and shared equally. We have no intention of creating jealousy by allocating resources in an unfair manner. That said, we don't really have any supplies at this point anyway, so—"

"Not community resources!" Galway snapped.

"Well, what then?" Fisher responded, puzzled.

"Resources in general—personal resources that could be put to better use. We have people in this neighborhood who have extra items they're not using."

"And if they want to donate them—"

"It doesn't matter whether they want to! What matters is that items are distributed to those who need them most. In other words, Mr. Fisher, since you can't seem to comprehend a simple concept, we take them."

"Who's we?" Fisher asked nervously.

"The community. But, as chairman, you would lead the initiative."

"I can't simply take personal belongings because others might need them more. I don't have the authority."

"The Board does, or it *will*, if we all decide it."

"Perhaps, but I hardly think—"

"That's quite clear at this point." Galway said. "What do you people do, anyway? This crisis calls for action!"

"I'd hardly call this a crisis, Ms. Galway, but—"

"Perhaps not for you, Mr. 'Chairman-of-the-Board-lives-in-one-of-the-biggest-houses-in-the-neighborhood' Fisher. You and your pal Bates with your housekeepers and butlers while the rest of us stumble around in dark houses. And I'll bet that's the case for all of you!" Galway finished, glaring at the figures seated onstage.

Fisher felt supremely uncomfortable. The last thing he needed was attention directed at his personal situation. He calculated his response to satisfy Galway while shifting the focus of the conversation.

"Ms. Galway, let me assure you that I care deeply about the members of this community and have worked tirelessly to make sure all are provided for in this, um, crisis. Your plan is novel in theory and broad in scope, so it will take some time to nail out the specifics in a satisfactory manner. Anyone else have anything to offer in the way of plans or ideas?"

The room was silent. The man yawned and checked his watch. He had always found Rose Galway a little pushy and a lot boring and wondered why his wife liked her. He shook himself and followed the other residents into the warm evening air.

Wednesday

*D*AMN IT, DAMN IT, DAMN IT! DAMN THIS BLASTED HOUSE AND *everything in it that won't work. Damn this dark, damn this stupid faucet. And damn yourself for being a fool.*

The man struggled to regain control of his temper. Standing half-asleep in a pitch-black bathroom made such a task difficult, especially after stubbing his toe on the doorframe.

That's what you get for not bringing your flashlight.

All made worse by this new problem of no running water.

&

"Why don't you go get some? I'm at work, remember?"

"So am I. Just because I work from home doesn't mean I'm always available. We have an online conference starting in twenty minutes with several potential donors. If anything, my work is more important to society than yours."

"Don't hit me with that moral argument crap! I provide most of the income, and you know it! I'm also swamped all day today."

"Then get some on the way home."

"By then, traffic will be terrible, and there probably won't be any left."

"Don't wait so long, then."

"I just told you I have no choice."

"Neither do I—in fact, I've got to go get ready for this call. Bye."

"No, wait—"

The line was dead. The man slipped the phone into his pocket and took a few deep breaths.

His phone buzzed. "About to start my call," the message read. "Got a text from R. Galway. Says another meeting scheduled for tonight, mandatory attendance. Just FYI since you'd probably miss the notification."

The man groaned. He hated everything—the stupid power outage, the water issue, his job, pointless community meetings, his wife's passive-aggressive behavior.

His phone rang. "What now?" he yelled without checking the caller ID.

"Uh, yeah, it's Joey—you finish that report yet?"

"Yes, sir, almost done."

∽

"Go inside, both of you. You're not helping. Daddy has to carry these heavy jugs inside and you're getting in his way."

"I can carry one!"

"No, you can't. They're bigger than you are. You and your sister together couldn't carry one. Now go inside, like I told you."

The kids pouted but obeyed. The man watched them go, feeling a bit guilty but glad he had controlled his boiling temper. He carried the jugs inside.

"Honey, what's for dinner?" The man had heard his wife approach and asked the question without looking up from arranging the jugs on the floor.

"I was going to ask you the same question."

The man stopped working and studied his wife, looking for any sign of sarcasm in her expression.

"You didn't order anything?"

"No, I've been busy. Besides, you don't always like what I get when I order for everyone. Remember a few months ago?"

"But that was because you bought Indian food for a football party!" The man paused, physically and mentally exhausted.

Can't think in this heat.

That gave him an idea—he'd make dinner outside.

The man hopped in his car and headed to the local grocery, soon returning with several bags and a gallon of lemonade. He ignored his wife's inquisitive look and went straight out to the back patio. She followed.

"What did you get?"

"Hot dogs and beef patties."

"Not very imaginative."

"I don't need a lecture right now. It's easy, they taste good, and the kids like them. Besides, grilling is therapeutic for me."

"Okay." She went back inside, holding the door open for the kids as they came out.

"You guys hungry? Bet you don't know what I got!"

"We know, Daddy," the girl said. "I don't want a hot dog, though."

"How about a patty?"

"No, not that either. I don't want to eat anything. My tummy is making funny noises."

"That's because you're hungry."

The girl shook her head stubbornly. "No, I'm not hungry."

"It'll be a few minutes before I get these cooked. You'll probably feel better by then. You're hungry, right?" he asked the boy.

"Uh-huh," the boy responded hesitantly.

The man turned on the gas, the kids watching silently.

They're sure quiet.

"Why don't you go inside while Daddy cooks?"

"It's hot inside."

That's true.

He looked at the grill.

Something's wrong.

The man picked up the propane tank and shook it.

Empty. I'll grab the other one.

He walked to the other end of the patio and stopped, not finding the tank in its usual place behind the potted plant.

"Kiddos, did you see the other propane tank the last time Daddy grilled? I think that was Friday."

"I saw it yesterday," the boy said. "Mommy sent me to play outside and my ball went in the plant. I saw the tank."

"Yesterday?"

"Uh-huh."

"Are you sure?"

"Yeah."

The man went inside and spoke to his wife, who had no information to offer. "He's probably confused," she said. "You must have moved it last time you cooked."

"No, I didn't. I'm careful—I always put it back."

"Because you never forget anything. Nothing like flashlights or important community meetings, for example."

"Leave it. I'm telling you, it wasn't me. I didn't even use that canister last time. I remember because I was busy talking to Kurt and never even went near it."

Wait.

"I wonder . . . maybe Kurt took the tank?"

"Kurt, next door? Why would he?"

"He was watching me grill. He mentioned something about fish he wanted to grill at some point, I think."

"So maybe he borrowed it."

"You can't borrow a perishable resource!" the man exploded, allowing a day's worth of pent-up frustration to boil over. "That's like borrowing a match or a paper towel. He took it, not borrowed!"

"You don't know that."

"Who else would have taken it?"

"I don't know. But what's the difference? Maybe he needed it more."

The man stormed back outside. He ignored the kids and marched over to the fence separating his yard from Kurt's.

Looking over the pool and yard, he spied a grill close by the house.

Was that there before?

No, he didn't think so. Kurt had said something about cleaning it.

Well, it's out now. And he's got a tank—my tank, I'll bet.

He went inside.

"I was right—he took it."

"Are you sure it's yours?"

"Yeah."

"How are you sure? Did you label it?"

"No, but—"

"So how do you know? And if you're so sure, why didn't you take it back?"

"Because . . . I figured I'd let him use it a bit longer."

"Uh-huh, sure. So, what are you going to do now? We still need food."

"I know, let me think for a second! Maybe if I—"

The door opened, and the boy entered, looking a little scared. "Crystal threw up, Daddy."

"She what?"

"She threw up. She had a tummy ache, and then she threw up. I think she's sick. And my tummy hurts too."

The man's wife bolted outside.

"Sit down here, son."

The boy sat, visibly pale. The girl entered with her mother, tears staining her face.

How the hell did this happen? Man, it's hot in here.

The man fanned himself with a newspaper he'd picked up from a nearby table.

His phone rang.

"What?"

"So, you coming?"

"Wait, who is . . . not a good time, Ryan. Am I coming to what?"

"The meeting—it's about to start! Better get over here." Ryan's voice sounded annoyingly cheerful. "I expect fireworks tonight, and you won't want to miss it. Not that you really have a choice, anyway. See ya' in a bit!"

The line went dead.

The man hurled his phone onto a nearby sofa.

ᔕᔐ

"Come on in, ladies and gentlemen, come right on in. Please find a chair—don't let the unfamiliar arrangement disturb you. We've got room for everyone. Don't be shy, come right on in."

The man groaned inwardly. Fisher's jovial eagerness heralded a long night ahead.

Where to sit?

Everything looked different. The table full of Board members remained on the stage up front, but the focus of the room had shifted to its center through a total restructuring of the seating layout. The chairs faced inward and wound their way in several rows from the left side of the stage to the right, hugging the sides of the room and looping around back to create a large oval-shaped space in the center of the rectangular hall. A small raised platform, currently occupied by the chairman, marked the center of this area. The man sat down in the rearmost row.

"Good evening again, everyone. I see most of you have found a seat. As I alluded to a minute ago, we have indeed altered the seating arrangement to allow for greater interaction in a more communal atmosphere. Unique times call for unique measures, and the Board is ready for action. Decisions have been made . . . and made quickly. To enlighten us concerning the conditions necessitating these decisions, please welcome Mr. Desmond Skates."

Skates left the table and made his way down to the platform.

"Yes, thank you. Tonight is going to be a full night, so let me just briefly lay out the details of our present situation. We have no water currently. For anyone wondering, this is true for all residents. As with the electrical issues, the areas surrounding our community do not appear to be affected.

"I'm sure the question now on everyone's mind is whether the power and water situations are linked. We believe so, but, at this point, we still lack the information needed to make a more definitive statement on that front. Just know we're diligently seeking answers and will continue to do so until everything is resolved. That's all I have. Are there any questions?"

Stony silence followed. One hand went up. Skates acknowledged a plump little man who sprang to his feet.

"So, are we just supposed to not use any water, then? No power and no water—how's that supposed to work?"

"I realize it's inconvenient—"

"Inconvenient! It's more than that, sir! Why, if I'd known about this before I moved here, I'd have had second thoughts! The whole reason I moved here was to avoid the problems of the Big City!"

"Yes, I understand, and I'd say that six straight years of no issues isn't a bad track record."

"I'm not talking about the past six years, I'm talking about right now!" the plump man retorted, red-faced and panting heavily. "What about right now?"

"I'm not sure what you expect me to say," Skates began timidly. "It's pretty clear—"

"What's clear, Mr. Skates," a shrill voice interrupted, "is that we need a brand-new approach to this situation. I'm not one to say I told you so, but I in fact did that just yesterday. Would you care to readdress the situation now that we've received a full display of the Board's incompetence?"

Fisher, still standing on the platform, quickly grabbed the microphone from the flustered Skates.

"Certainly, Ms. Galway! In fact, we have considered last night's proposals, and the unforeseen and drastic changes that have taken place since that time have helped the Board recognize the merits of the system you proposed. We have devised a plan which will surely meet with your approval and that of the community as a whole."

"What decisions have been made, Mr. Fisher?" Rose Galway now stood in front of her chair in the first row.

"That will be explained shortly. At this point, however, I'd like to keep us on track by making sure Mr. Skates can conclude his remarks. Desmond, anything else to add?"

Skates merely shook his head before stepping off the platform and making his way back to the safety of his chair.

"Thank you, Desmond. Everyone here should have a pretty good idea of the current situation. The first rule of solving a problem is to identify the problem, which we've done. Now we can discuss the Board's decisions moving forward. To that end, please once again welcome Ms. Amber Richmond to discuss the details of our community action plan."

"Good evening! I know everyone is ready for action—I can feel excitement in the air!"

Nope.

"The Board shall not disappoint. With the aid of some helpful residents, we have devised a plan that will ensure everyone in our community is prepared to deal with this crisis. I've been tasked with taking an inventory of our available resources so we know where things stand. Later tonight, an email will go out containing a mandatory survey to be completed by tomorrow night's meeting."

Another meeting?

"Please use this survey to record your household's resources so the Board can determine where they can be allocated for best use.

"That's really all I have at the moment . . . any questions before we proceed with implementation details?"

Multiple hands shot up at once in a crowd now buzzing with scores of voices, the tumult only dying down as a flabby middle-aged man wearing a football jersey began speaking.

"So let me get this straight. We've got this problem, right? And in order to deal with it we have to complete some mandatory paperwork listing out all our stuff? And it's all so other people can take it? Count me out."

Several exclamations of approval as well as a few indignant rebukes came from the crowd.

Dissension in the ranks! This is getting interesting.

Amber Richmond smiled nervously. "I'm sorry our plan doesn't meet with your approval, Mr. . . . uh, sir, but we've done the best we can. As to counting you out, as you expressed it, I'm afraid we need one hundred percent support—"

"The name's Rogers, Hank Rogers. You don't need my support, and even if you did, you wouldn't get it. I don't need anyone telling me what to do with my own property!"

"I understand, Mr. Rogers, but it has been determined that compliance is both essential and required. If you'd like to discuss—"

"Required? And just how does that work? Are you threatening me? You can't make me do anything . . . I live here and you have no right . . ."

As the sputtering newcomer paused to catch his breath, Fisher took advantage of the delay to grab the microphone from the beleaguered Richmond.

"I think we're getting ahead of ourselves here," he said amiably. "I'd like to invite Mr. Tim Barlette up to discuss the regulatory aspects of this new endeavor. Tim?"

Amber Richmond made a quick escape back to the table as Barlette mounted the platform. Rogers collapsed into his chair, still breathing heavily.

"Thank you, Lawrence. So the basic outline has been provided, ladies and gentlemen."

Uh, not really.

"It's now my job to discuss the regulatory nature of the plan. My role as community regulations compliance manager involves monitoring community support for and compliance with the plan.

"All residents enjoy the benefits of secluded, private living in a safe community perfectly suited to suburban excellence. Along with benefits come responsibilities, and the most important obligation each individual has is to those around him. We Board members have been elected by all of you to represent your interests and develop policies that benefit the community as a whole. You put your trust in us, and now it's our turn to rely on each of you.

"To that end, we expect all residents to participate in the plan of their own volition. More details will be shared shortly, but, in the meantime, please trust that our expert analysis has foreseen any and all difficulties and provided contingencies for these situations. We've saved you all time and effort—all you have to do is follow the directions we provide. That said, the plan will only be effective if everyone plays a part.

"I'm sure some will ask if this is required," he continued. "That mindset is itself a problem—people sharing a community should not be asking if goodness toward their neighbors is mandated. We should all want to help others whether or not we are required to do so. That said, there are no official statutes or regulations being imposed on anyone here. When Ms. Richmond said participation is required, she of course meant required for the plan to work properly. I have no doubt all residents will contribute their fair share. No rules or requirements will be necessary—nobody needs the Board or the Homeowners' Association making life unpleasant. I believe we can best achieve our goals by encouraging cooperation through social pressure. People monitoring each other rather than us monitoring them. Community coercion beats coercion of the community any day!"

Barlette chuckled. No one else laughed.

"What does this mean, exactly? Well, it simply means we will hold each other accountable, thus eliminating the need for regulatory mandates. Remind your neighbors of their responsibilities so we can all get through this crisis safely and comfortably.

"Hopefully any confusion has now been cleared up."

Again, not really.

"I believe that Amber had—"

An initially subdued murmuring swelled into a cacophony of voices throughout the hall. Fisher preemptively cut in.

"Friends," he began affably, "just hold on a moment. All your questions will be answered. To save time and cut to the heart of the matter, those wishing to view the entire plan can do so on our community website. Also, I believe we have flyers outlining the basics of the plan which will now be distributed. Please take one from the stack and pass the rest along."

The man waited for the documents to make their way around his row. Taking a flyer, he began reading.

"The Plan—A Model for Community Interaction, Mutual Support, and Strategic Redistribution," the heading ran.

"Point 1: The supervising of all community resources by the Board."

Okay . . .

"Point 2: Community resources are those deemed as vital to communal functionality and well-being."

Meaning what exactly?

"Point 3: Distribution of collected resources will be based on perceived need within the community."

Yes, but . . .

"Point 4: Residents are encouraged to support this initiative by reporting any apparent negligence or nonadherence to the Board for review."

Seems excessive . . .

A sharp jab between the shoulder blades made him turn around.

"Ryan! You startled me. Where've you been?"

"I've been standing in the back. You read it yet?"

"Yup. You think it makes sense?"

"Oh yeah, I'm fully on board. Primed and ready for action! It'll be good for the community as a whole. Plus, I might find it useful myself." Ryan grinned.

"What do you mean?"

"Nothing, just that now's the time to address some long-standing inequity issues."

"I'm not sure what you're talking about, but you'd better find a seat. Looks like Fisher is about to start blabbing again."

"Take it easy on him," Ryan responded gaily. "He's doing his best. Well, so long until later."

✢

"Friends," Fisher began, "I'd like to move things along as quickly as possible for the sake of time. Anyone with questions can . . ."

Many hands instantly shot up.

". . . hold those questions until later. You've now all familiarized yourselves with the essential details of the plan."

The chairman paused, considering how to wrap things up quickly without providing opportunity for consolidated opposition to arise. An idea struck him. Make them choose a side. Ask them directly.

"At this point, I'd ask everyone who still opposes the plan to come take a seat up front." Fisher indicated the innermost row of the oval.

Nobody moved. Fisher waited several more seconds. Suddenly, the noise of a chair being pushed back drew his attention to Mike Bracken approaching the platform. Bracken, seeing no open seats in the designated row, halted several feet short of the platform before casting a questioning glance at Fisher. The chairman eyed him coldly and turned to the closest audience members.

"Friends, this gentleman is our first dissenter and requires a chair. Could one of you please make way for him? That is, of course, unless every one of you in this first row is also a dissenter."

Open seats appeared as if by magic.

Clever. Everyone likes to bitch until forced to take a stand. And now, Bracken's all by himself . . . no, wait . . . here comes Football Man. Got his breath back, I guess. A few more now . . . they just needed a leader. Still, not enough to give Fisher any problems.

Fisher clearly had the same thought.

"Ladies and gentlemen," he began, "my goal tonight was to conduct the necessary business of this meeting with all the efficiency and speed in my power. I know how busy we all are, especially in these trying times. Unfortunately, not everyone is yet willing to join us in our new endeavor. Perhaps we were too optimistic—too reliant on the simple hope of all coming together in pursuit of a common goal. As chairman of the Board, it's my duty to assume the good intentions of my fellow man, but such a mindset becomes difficult to maintain in the face of blatant disregard for community cohesion. That's what we are, after all—a community. I pride myself, however, on being open-minded, so I'm willing to hear the alternate viewpoint from those to whom empathy is merely a suggestion rather than a way of life."

Dang.

"Now, friends, let us acknowledge our differences by hearing from those few who disagree with our practical approach.

I'd like to invite our dissenters to share their reasons for opposing this community endeavor. Let's start by hearing from . . ."

Mike Bracken, sitting directly in front of Fisher, started to stand up.

". . . you sir," Fisher concluded, pointing at Hank Rogers, who hesitated before finally dragging his not-insignificant bulk toward the platform. Fisher smiled pleasantly and handed the mic down.

"Uh, hullo. First off, I'd like to apologize for my outburst earlier—I get sort of pissed off sometimes, and, well . . . as my wife'll tell you, I don't always keep my head screwed on straight. Anyway . . . now that I've had the chance to calm down a bit, the plan seems more reasonable, especially since it ain't mandatory. Not really, at least. I plan on helping out voluntarily. There won't be no need to remind me of my responsibilities like your paper mentioned."

Rogers wiped perspiration from his face.

"Well, that's about all I've got to say," he concluded. "No issues here—I just got upset with how fast all this was pushed through, but I'm better now. That's all I've got."

Fisher, smiling magnanimously, took the mic as Rogers squished back toward his seat.

One down.

"Thank you, Mr. Rogers. I'm glad to see you've joined the rest of us. Feel free to take a seat further back so you're no longer in the first row. That's right—anywhere you'd like. You see folks, a simple apology, and all is forgiven. Harmony restored. Mr. Rogers has illustrated how we can all align our individual viewpoints with those of the greater whole."

"May I add some brief thoughts?"

The entire room, Fisher included, looked around for the source of the shrill voice. Rose Galway had somehow managed to approach the platform unobserved.

"Of course, Ms. Galway. Folks, allow me to introduce Ms. Rose Galway, a key leader in an initiative which she herself first suggested. Ms. Galway, please proceed with your remarks."

Just keep them short. And no preaching.

"Let me start by echoing the chairman's commendation," she began. "Mr. Rogers is to be lauded for his apology. I was deeply moved by his public change of heart to the extent that I felt the need to acknowledge him openly. That's all I wanted to say, but while I'm up here, I'll just touch on a few other items."

Go ahead, might as well . . .

"First, I am deeply honored to be leading this initiative. Second, I believe the plan will help create justice and fairness in a community currently plagued by marked inequity and individualism. To that end, I must say I'm ashamed and disgusted by the level of selfishness exhibited by the dissenters. An appropriate name, though I'd use the word 'agitators' myself."

She glared at the few remaining objects of her indignation.

"However, as an open-minded person, I will voice no further objections during tonight's discussion." She turned to Fisher. "I yield the rest of my time."

Yield the—what is this, Congress?

Fisher took the mic. "Thank you, Ms. Galway. We're all grateful for your leadership and example. Now, to resume our friendly debate here. Ma'am, would you care to share your concerns?"

Fisher gestured to a startled redhead seated in the front row. The woman shifted uncomfortably in her chair and adjusted her glasses before rising and slowly approaching the platform.

"Ahem, excuse me. First off, I'd just like to state that I don't exactly oppose the plan. My husband was too busy to attend tonight and asked me to come, so here I am. His name is Josh. I'm Jill—Jill Hackworth. We've got two young kids at their grandparents' right now. Anyway, I'm not trying to cause trouble, and now I'm almost ashamed to be standing here, but I felt I needed to say something . . . for some reason I just have a bad feeling . . . I'm speaking on behalf of my husband and what I think he'd say. It just seems a bit much to have official plans, particularly when all the neighbors I know would cheerfully help others of their own free will. Please don't get me wrong. I'm not saying it's a bad idea, per se . . . I still don't really understand what it involves . . . well, at this point, I'm just rambling . . . I think I'd better sit down."

Jill Hackworth abashedly thrust the microphone into Fisher's hands and fled toward a new seat further back.

Two down.

Fisher spoke. "Let's be kind, friends—I heard some snickering just now. Remember, we're all in this together.

Ms. Hackworth is merely looking out for the interests of her husband, which I'm sure she now understands to be the same as the interests of the community." The chairman paused. "Now . . . let's see who we've got left. Why don't we hear from you now, sir?"

As the new speaker approached the platform, the man noticed his familiar features for the first time.

Wait, what the—

Kurt took the microphone with an air of enthusiasm not displayed by his predecessors.

"Hi, everyone!"

What do you think you're doing?

"First off, I think this whole community thing is super rad. It's awesome to see everyone coming together like this. I'm Kurt, by the way."

Yes, I know.

"Anyway, I'm a bit out of the loop here—super busy all the time. Seems like we've got a good system. I'm pretty chill, but as I just said, I'm crazy busy right now, and I won't be able to participate . . . but I wanted to make sure everyone knew it's not because I've got any problems or whatever. I'm not a dissenter, if that's the term. I'm guessing there are some other people in a similar sort of position, so I just wanted to put in a good word for them, too. Anyway, that's all I've got!"

Rose Galway stood up.

"We're all busy, sir, but we find ways to help those in need. You're young and intelligent and should have little difficulty complying with these new directives."

"He's just lazy!" yelled a middle-aged woman from across the oval. "I've got kids and a house to take care of, and I'm not complaining. Here you are, with no screaming children, no constant housework, nothing! My kids were so hot last night they didn't fall asleep until two in the morning. If I can comply with the plan, so can you!"

She sat down. Kurt looked surprised but managed to reply.

"No, I assure you, I do want to help. I'll help as best I can— we still haven't been told what kind of help is needed—I just want everyone to understand why I won't be around enough to really get involved. I don't need help, and I certainly don't want to take anything from anyone."

The man suddenly found himself standing.

"So you don't want to take anything for yourself?"

Kurt's gaze found the man. "Oh, hey, how's it going? What was your question?"

"I said you don't want to take anything from anybody?"

"No, of course not."

"That's interesting, as I have direct evidence to the contrary. You care to retract that statement before I let everyone in on the secret?"

"Uh, I'm not sure what you mean, but—"

"How about a hint? Does the word propane ring any bells?"

"Propane?"

"Specifically, *my* propane?"

"What about it?"

"Maybe the fact that it's missing? Now, who could have taken it? Not you, by any chance?"

"Oh yeah, as a matter of fact . . . I was going to tell you—"

"I knew it!" The man addressed the crowd. "Kurt's my next-door neighbor, and the other day he just took my propane tank without even asking. He's already taken my stuff without permission, and now he's acting like he wants to help others!"

Kurt showed visible surprise at his neighbor's unexpected antagonism.

"Hang on, man, chill out for a second! I thought we were cool, you and me! I was going to bring it back, even replace it if necessary . . . I thought you were cool with that, based on our conversation the other day, but I guess I misunderstood . . ."

"No misunderstanding! I never promised anything—you just took!" The man felt himself getting angrier the more he thought about it.

"Okay, I get it, I get it . . . everyone's digging the plan and we're going ahead with it. Again, I just wanted—"

"You wanted to get out of your responsibility!" a voice called out. Others joined in. A few rose from their chairs, and the entire room quickly erupted in confused shouting.

The man sat down. He watched Kurt, turning this way and that in a futile attempt to address accusers on all sides.

Need to get hold of myself. Got too angry . . . now, look!

A couple minutes elapsed before Fisher managed to quiet the crowd and get everyone seated. Kurt was gone. The man noticed the front row completely empty, save for one chair. Mike Bracken sat calmly as before.

∽

"Well, now, friends, that was exciting, wasn't it? Certainly gets the blood pumping! I speak facetiously, of course. We're all adults who must remember to treat each other with sympathy and respect, even those who oppose our efforts to help others. Speaking of which, our plan has clearly won new converts." Fisher waved his arm around the oval. "Observe! Our friends and neighbors have all joined forces as one! Let us now proceed with the closing details of this meeting."

About time!

Mike Bracken slowly stood up and looked at Fisher, who carefully avoided his gaze.

"Final items . . . let's see . . ."

"Excuse me."

Fisher glanced up from his notes, his reluctant gaze finally resting on Bracken. "Yes?"

"I have not yet been able to speak."

"What's your name?"

"Bracken, Mike."

"Well, Mr. Bracken, it looks like you're the only person intent on holding up the proceedings. Are you sure what you have to say is urgent enough to keep these good people waiting even longer?"

"I don't want to keep anyone waiting—that's why I was the first up here."

"Very well. Friends, please give Mr. Bracken your undivided attention for the next few minutes, and then I'll wrap things up."

Please do.

Bracken took the proffered mic and addressed the crowd.

"Hello, I'm Mike. I'll try to be as brief as possible here, but I feel obligated to explain my decision concerning the plan, as it's called. The last thing I generally want to do is attract attention to myself or my family."

Fail.

"We tend to handle things on our own, as some of you might have noticed. I do, however, strongly believe in developing a sense of community, which is why we want to get to know more of you personally. We want to meet you, and we want our kids to get to know your kids. We've also been looking for worthwhile community activities in which to take part. Which brings me to this new initiative. I regret that my first interaction with a community endeavor must be a contrarian one, but I don't believe I have any other options at this point.

"Crises call for serious action. What we're looking at here is not a crisis. An annoyance, yes. A frustrating and inconvenient set of circumstances? Yes. Even a complete logistical mess? Yes, of course. I wouldn't dream of denying it. But these are problems which can be overcome without significant cost or labor expenditure. We live minutes away from superstores stocked with supplies. We can have food and water delivered. We can order online. No disaster has occurred, no houses blown down, no homes flooded, no health crisis, no apocalypse. I say all this not to make light of our situation but to remind everyone that action starts at the individual level. As head of my household, I know what's best for my family. The same applies to all of you, as situations differ from household to household."

Get to the point.

"All that said, the plan concerns me. It concerns me because it forces families to look to the interests of others rather than their own. It is not the position of any group to direct an individual's actions toward philanthropic endeavors, especially in the browbeating manner I've seen tonight. I am ready and willing to help out where possible, but I refuse to be pressured into taking any actions with regard to my own resources.

"To close, I support a desire to assist others, but I will be doing so in my own way, not as part of the plan."

Complete silence. Rose Galway sprang from her chair.

"I find it highly ironic, Mr. Bracken, that you spoke of wanting to help people but then immediately refused to do so. I suppose you only want to help others if it's convenient? As a leader of this project, I take your statement as a direct and personal insult!"

Bracken shrugged.

"As I said before, I am in fact willing to help others. But it will be at my discretion, and my charity will not be dictated by others."

"Charity, Mr. Bracken, is mandated in order—"

"Charity cannot be mandated, Ms. Galway. It's voluntary. That's what makes it charity. If it's not voluntary, it's not charity."

"That's not true! Charity is defined by your intentions and your heart—if you seek to help people, all steps taken to achieve that goal constitute acts of charity."

"Those actions might be commendable, but they are not charity, Ms. Galway. Not if they're mandatory or the result of social pressure."

"Say what you like, Mr. Bracken, but you are willfully preventing us from using your resources for charitable purposes."

"You cannot be charitable with my things. I can because they belong to me."

"I have no intention of taking lessons in charity from you, sir!" Rose Galway snorted, drawing a few sympathetic exclamations from a largely supportive crowd. "No sense of community! Groups are and should be the focus of all decision-making. Mr. Bracken, do you at least agree that the group is the most important thing here?"

"I do not. I think the individual is most important."

Figures.

"The individual?!" Galway was shocked. "More important than the group?"

"Yes."

"But how could you think individuals are more important than an entire group?"

Bracken eyed her calmly. "Because, ma'am, groups consist of individuals. By strengthening the individual, we ultimately strengthen the group. Group-focused systems only look out for an individual's needs if those needs happen to fit in with those of the group."

"That's just mistrustful conjecture!" Galway retorted. "You assume the group doesn't care about its own members and that human beings won't act out of inherent benevolence and goodness."

"That's because he doesn't believe in goodness!"

Ms. Perkins stood among the crowd, hands on her hips and a look of indignation on her face.

"It's true!" she continued vehemently. "Just the other day, he told several of us he doesn't think people are good. He also said everybody is capable of doing terrible, evil things. Made it seem like we're all a bunch of psychopaths waiting to unleash our fury on the world. It was shameful! And now I see why he talks that way—he thinks himself better than all of us!"

Bracken glanced at Fisher, but the chairman remained mute, content to let public sentiment do the dirty work.

"I don't think I'm better than anyone. I simply think human beings are flawed and that their decisions, even made as a group, can be flawed as well."

"At least we're doing something!" Perkins snapped. "Personally, I try to go above and beyond whatever is required of me; for example, I'm donating grocery store gift cards to this effort in addition to my share of resources."

"Donating to whom?"

"The community, Mr. Bracken."

"Yes, but to whom, specifically?"

"Whoever needs it."

"But who needs it? If anyone's dying of hunger, I've got actual food in storage."

"I'm sure someone less fortunate than myself can be found."

"Undoubtedly, but, going back to my earlier point, we're not in dire straits here. This isn't a crisis, and everyone in this neighborhood is financially stable. Our community is the only one affected, so no homeless or poverty-stricken individuals will be receiving this aid. What exactly, then, is the point of all this?"

Rose Galway cut in before Perkins could reply.

"The point, Mr. Bracken, is not whether you think the plan makes sense but whether you have a desire to help others. Based on your comments, the answer is no. I think we're done here."

"Fine with me." Bracken addressed the crowd. "If anyone needs help setting up a power source, I've got a little expertise in that area. Just come by the house."

The audience remained silent as Bracken started for his seat.

Finally!

"Mr. Bracken."

Bracken stopped and turned toward Fisher. "Yes?"

"I'm glad Ms. Galway has saved us all some time by cutting this unfruitful dialogue short, but please understand that the Board has implemented the plan and expects full cooperation."

Bracken nodded. "Yup, I understand all right; I'm just not willing to go along with it."

"But you have to."

"No, you said it wasn't mandatory. Even if it was, I wouldn't participate."

"It's not mandatory, per se, but please remember that those who run afoul of the Board's good graces tend to find the consequences rather inconvenient."

"Then I'll face the consequences."

Fisher took a deep breath. "Mr. Bracken, I'm afraid this discussion has taken up too much time already. I'm sorry you have feelings so directly contrary to the well-being of our residents. Time is running short, however, so I suggest you go home and consider what I've said in preparation for tomorrow night's meeting."

Bracken merely shrugged and walked back to his seat.

The chairman addressed the crowd. "I'm afraid we're out of time, folks. I trust we can pick up here tomorrow with fewer disruptions. Have a good evening!"

Hallelujah!

Thursday

So damn tired. Every few minutes, it's Daddy, I feel sick again. Throw up in the toilet, not on the . . . floor. Nice. At least it wasn't the rug. What, you did it there, too? Your room? Just not in the bed. Oh, please no. Strip sheets, disinfect, can't do laundry. Rug smells foul. Then do it all over again. In the toilet, damn it! What's so difficult to understand? Don't yell at them, honey, you're their father. And you're my wife, but you still yell at me all the time. So freaking hot. Open the windows. Generator noise. More cleaning, more puking, more cleaning. Almost morning. Leave for work.

The man had taken an early lunch after a completely unproductive morning. He now sat alone, mechanically chewing a sandwich. His phone buzzed.

His wife texted that she'd completed the survey and that the propane tank had reappeared. The man smiled weakly. Any bit of joy was welcome, and remembering his masterful takedown of his presumptuous neighbor brightened his spirits.

I told him off—won't have any trouble next time! Next time. Another meeting tonight.

The man groaned.

❧

The mayor was present. Few residents knew him. Many had never even seen him, and most considered him a figurehead who let the Board conduct community affairs. They now eyed him skeptically, surprised they had elected as mayor a balding, corpulent man who sat fanning himself onstage.

Fisher had started the meeting by apologizing profusely for the lack of air conditioning. "Some unforeseen problem—inexcusable, really!"

The building was hot, and tempers were even hotter. The man felt the tension the moment he arrived. He could barely restrain his own frustration from boiling over, having just left a house occupied by a dictatorial spouse and two emaciated children. Fisher was talking, but the man wasn't listening. His gaze wandered from Fisher's platform to the stage and the table full of Board members.

And Rose Galway. And the mayor. All sweaty in that suit.

The chairman handed the microphone to Amber Richmond.

"Thank you, Lawrence. As outreach coordinator, I have reviewed the surveys received today. I'm working closely with Mr. Skates, our resources director, to determine proper allocation. Hopefully, everyone noticed a section at the end of the survey providing an option to claim a hardship case. We received eight responses in total. The Board has determined the resources pledged will be sufficient for five households. Since this is a community endeavor, the Board believes the community should decide for itself who will receive these resources. To that end, we will now allow those who submitted a claim to make their case publicly."

Richmond glanced at her notes. "First up, please welcome Ms. Rachel Peak."

A middle-aged blonde timidly approached the platform.

"Uh, hello, everyone. I really didn't expect anything like this—I had no idea we'd be sharing everything openly. I was just trying to ease my family's situation a bit. My husband's been sick for two weeks now and has some underlying medical issues. I work full time with three kids, and trying to take care of them and my husband is becoming increasingly difficult. The house is so hot now, I'm worried for my husband with his fever. That's all, really—any supplies provided would allow me to stay home and help."

She stopped and looked at Amber Richmond, who smiled politely and retrieved the microphone. Rachel Peak hurriedly returned to her seat.

"Next, we have Mr. James Ingland," Richmond continued. "I'm going to keep this moving, folks, for the sake of time."

Ingland, a rather dumpy-looking man wearing a garish plum blazer, addressed the crowd.

"Yes, well, I've got a case to make," he began rather loudly. *Calm down.*

"Not for me—it's for my wife. As a man of means, I generally look out for myself. Always have, always will. However, my wife has a long history of bad headaches and migraines, and this lack of A/C is just killing her. I have no time to see to her needs, so I figured the community could help my poor little wife. It's about time something got done around here."

Amber Richmond smiled politely. "I assure you, sir, we're doing our best. Thank you for sharing. All right, next we have Ms. Jane Yancy."

"I believe my situation is the most important."

Bold start.

"My husband has been ill for several years. A unique condition, according to the medical experts. Very exhausting and expensive treatments. Not that we lack resources—we are secure financially! I have two children who both require devoted attention and care from me personally, as no caretaker has been able to handle their exceptional talent and general exuberance. It takes an extreme amount of dedication and energy, and my hormonal imbalances don't make it any easier. Far be it from me to complain, however. I never ask others to share my burdens, and I hesitated to even submit a request. Now that I've seen the competition, however, I regret my initial hesitation. Frankly, I'd be embarrassed to request resources were I to find myself in such petty circumstances as my predecessors. Each to his own, however. I think—"

"You're full of it!" James Ingland shouted, standing in the crowd. "People like you don't give two turds about my wife or anyone like her! It's just look at me, I'm so important, my family is perfect, give me stuff because I deserve it. I'm sick of it!"

Great, here we go.

Jane Yancy quickly assumed a scornful expression. "Oh, poor you!" she sneered. "Let's all feel sorry for Willy Wonka—his wife has headaches. Such a catastrophe! The worst disaster to ever befall a human being. Why don't we just ignore the legitimate needs of the entire community so we can address his selfish desires?"

"Easy for you to say!" Ingland shot back. "You're here to get stuff for yourself—I'm looking after my wife. If you're so perfect, figure stuff out for yourself!"

"How about you follow your own advice?!" Yancy retorted. "Your problems are minor compared to mine. I'm the biggest victim here, and, as such, I deserve consideration!"

"You think you're a victim?" a new speaker shouted from the crowd. "My wife passed away just four months ago, and I've been trying to single parent two kids while working full time. You've got it easy! Spare me your sackcloth and ashes routine!"

Another voice. "That's right! What makes all of you so special? Why, my family—"

The room erupted into general chaos and commotion. People shouting over each other, mocking, agreeing, disagreeing, cheering. Few remained sitting.

Amber Richmond and Fisher stood on the central platform vainly attempting to quiet the crowd. The chairman, disgusted with his lack of success and the volatility of his audience, eventually dropped his gaze and noticed Mike Bracken standing calmly before the platform. In a moment,

Bracken had mounted the platform and addressed the suddenly attentive audience.

"Thank you, everyone," he began. "I did not plan on speaking tonight, but this descent into chaos has prompted me to offer what I believe to be the simplest and most straightforward solution. As I see it, we are all upset at each other for no reason."

No reason? Easy to say when you've got power.

"To that end, please allow me a few minutes to outline a solution."

"Ms. Peak?" Bracken searched the crowd. "Ah, there you are! Ms. Peak, it occurs to me that your situation would be improved should your A/C be restored for your husband's sake, correct?"

"Yes."

"Great—I can provide some assistance in that area. If you supply the financial means required, I will assist with the technical aspects. That goes for Mr. Ingland as well. Ms. Yancy, for your unique situation I will have to defer to the expertise of my wife, who happens to be highly trained in working with children, even those who might be somewhat . . . difficult. I'm sure she'd be willing to watch them during the day while—"

This was too much for Jane Yancy, who popped out of her chair like a jack-in-the-box.

"I don't need your demeaning offer of charity!" she stormed. "Leave my little angels in the care of your wife? What makes her such a childcare expert? I've seen your brood of rascals, and they don't hold a candle to my darlings. I ask you to mind your own business, sir, and that directly!"

Woah. Never mention the kids.

"I had no intention of offending you, ma'am—I'm simply trying to help restore peace." Bracken paused before addressing the entire audience. "My other offers still stand, and I'll help anyone else who needs it."

Ms. Peak stood up. "I'd very much appreciate your giving us a hand," she said gratefully. "We just need the house cool for my husband. We'll cover the expense if you'll handle the rest."

"Sure—that's what I'm here for. No use having a big fight. I'll get to work on it tomorrow. Thanks, everyone."

Bracken stepped off the platform.

"Mr. Bracken."

Bracken paused and turned round to face a now-composed Fisher.

Woke up, have we?

"Mr. Bracken, I must remind you of several items. First, the plan has already been implemented, and it would be a waste of time and resources to backtrack now."

"Better than continuing to waste—"

"This is not up for discussion, Mr. Bracken. It is not your place to critique the efficacy of the Board's decisions. Undermining a community endeavor for personal reasons will not be tolerated. Any arrangements you make with your neighbors must necessarily be outside the realm and scope of this project. Group meetings are not the place to discuss your own private affairs."

"Agreed, which is why—"

"And lastly, I'm afraid we must address the elephant in the room here. I'm sure everyone remembers our little discussion last night? It pains me to mention this, but before you can expect to interact with your neighbors, you must be willing to pledge your support to our community initiative. We must all have skin in the game. You've had time to think it over—will you support the plan?"

"No, I support individual decision-making."

"Mr. Bracken, the Board has the power to make life very tedious for those who disobey its directives."

"I'm well aware of that."

"Well, that's on you, then," Fisher concluded. "Expect to hear from us. I refuse to waste any more of our valuable time."

"What about his stuff?"

"Pardon?" Fisher searched the crowd for the new speaker.

"His stuff." A middle-aged man wearing khaki shorts and a polo stood up. "His resources—the ones owed to the community."

"What about them?"

"Does he have to contribute? It's all well and fine to have the Board issue a reprimand or something, but that won't help any of us. I'm a widower trying to take care of a couple kids. Name's Thacker, by the way."

"You do have a point, Mr. Thacker," Fisher observed. "Penalties punish the crime, but they don't ease the suffering of the victims. Further action must be taken. Do you have any suggestions?"

Thacker responded without hesitation. "The generator—the damn generator! Make him turn that thing off if he's too selfish to give it to someone who needs it more!"

Hear, hear! There's something I can get behind!

Fisher considered. "That seems reasonable, given the circumstances. Disruptions of that nature are not conducive to community welfare. Mr. Bracken, do you understand the nature of the complaint against you?"

"Mr. Thacker doesn't care for the noise," Bracken responded simply. "I get that—not much I can do about it, though."

"It's not the noise!" Thacker responded vehemently. "I mean, that's part of it, but the main thing is that . . . the real issue . . . well, I just don't see why you should be allowed to have that thing going while everyone else suffers without power."

"I've already offered to help others get the same system set up," Bracken noted.

"That's irrelevant."

"No, I think it's perfectly relevant."

"I say it isn't!"

Fisher intervened. "Mr. Bracken, kindly refrain from contradicting the current speaker. He has raised an important issue, and it's one you must address directly."

"I'm still trying to understand the nature of the complaint. Is the noise the problem, or is it something else?"

Thacker broke in loudly. "The noise is *a* problem, but it's not *the* problem. I can live with noise, but I can't live around someone heartless enough to enjoy comfort while the rest of us suffer."

"Are they suffering because of me? Something I've done?"

"I'm talking about the general suffering everyone is experiencing. Everyone but you, it seems."

"How would turning off my generator alleviate the suffering of others?"

"It's obvious! I wouldn't—we wouldn't—have to experience suffering not shared by everyone around us. We're all in this together! How would you feel if you experienced hardship on your own?"

"I would feel unprepared and foolish for my lack of foresight."

"What's that supposed to mean?"

Fisher stepped in. "No insults, please, gentlemen. Let me cut to the chase here. Mr. Bracken, will you voluntarily shut down your generator?"

"Due to the noise?"

"That's not the issue at present . . ."

"So, what is? I still haven't received an answer on that point."

"It disrupts community sentiments, Mr. Bracken. We cannot foster a spirit of unity if one individual acts on his own."

"Turning off my generator helps nobody. It hurts the family I've worked in advance to protect and forces them to suffer because others are envious and unprepared."

The crowd gave voice to indignant disagreement.

Bad move, dude—everyone already hates you.

"That's enough," Fisher replied curtly. "I'm directing our Board to draw up an official cease and desist order via our Homeowners' Association under Mr. Tim Barlette's guidance. You are hereby ordered to turn off your generator, effective tomorrow. A formal written notice will follow for the sake of procedure, but you have received a verbal directive and must act accordingly."

Boom.

The entire hall buzzed with voices, many residents clapping loudly. Bracken, still standing halfway between the central platform and the audience, merely shrugged.

"I'm going home to my family."

And then he was gone.

Good riddance! Just wasting everyone's time. We're all angry. And hot. Damn.

The man wiped sweat from his brow as he watched the fat mayor attempt to fan himself only to stop a few moments later, panting from the exertion.

⁓

"Well, friends, it's been an exciting evening, and we're just getting started. Rest assured, the Board will analyze the individual cases presented earlier to determine how to distribute available resources in the most equitable manner. We will provide updates as necessary, but, for now, we must move on with a discussion about enforcement, led by Mr. Tim Barlette."

Barlette mounted the platform. "Thank you, Lawrence. Enforcement. Yes, I know that's a harsh word. Nobody likes to talk about it, but sometimes situations arise that necessitate such discussions. I need not provide any illustration beyond what you have just witnessed. One person found our community guidelines inconvenient, and we had no choice but to step in with authority. Neither Mr. Fisher nor myself enjoys taking such measures, but we do it for the safety and health of our community.

"To that end, we need to offer an open forum for the sharing of any grievances or violations of the plan. Due to time constraints, this period will be brief. Please introduce yourself, state your concern, and then wait patiently for the individual in question to respond. We've got about twenty minutes, folks. If you wish to speak, please raise your hand and I'll call you up."

Waste of time. Why bring up issues? I wouldn't. Except for Kurt, but that's different . . .

Barlette handed the mic to a young woman standing in front of the platform.

"Thank you, Mr. Barlette," she began. "My name is Megan Bradley, and my family has resided in this community for a year and a half now. I take no pleasure in what I'm about to do, but I feel obligated for the sake of the community. My next-door neighbor has unfortunately failed to—"

An exclamation from the crowd cut her off.

"Don't listen to her!" another woman in her early thirties yelled. "Don't listen—it's all nonsense! She'll tell you I've been saving items for my family. It's not true! Yes, I have several coolers in our garage, which Megan Bradley has no doubt seen on many occasions. I knew she was spying, even before all this started! We have coolers, ice chests, and several other food storage items. Fact is, they're not ours. They belong to extended family who left them with us temporarily. They're not ours to offer. Mind your own business!" she finished, casting a furious glance at Bradley before turning to reprimand a young girl squirming in the seat beside her.

With her assailant preoccupied, Bradley gathered her wits and counterattacked.

"I'm not a spy! I'm simply a concerned citizen, and I know better than anyone, Mandy Reynolds, the sort of games you play!"

"You're just upset because last month I reported you for letting your cat do its business in my yard!"

Wonderful, a neighborhood spat.

"That's got nothing to do with it," Bradley shot back. "I just know the sort of games you play to escape responsibility, and I don't want the neighborhood to suffer because of it. No one has any means of storing food, and you conveniently forgot to report those massive coolers to the resources committee."

"I've already explained that! I think you—"

Barlette snatched the microphone from Bradley. "Ladies, let's calm down a minute. I'm sure we can find a way to resolve this peacefully. If there's a third party we could ask . . . "

"*She* knows!" Megan Bradley exclaimed, pointing to her adversary's little girl. "Patsy, whose coolers are those in your garage?"

The girl looked up at the sound of her name, but her mother interjected.

"That's not right!" she exclaimed. "You can't drag my child into this!"

"Calm down please, Ms. Reynolds. I don't see the harm. Patsy?" Barlette addressed the child, who looked at him inquisitively. "Patsy, can you answer Ms. Bradley's question? Are those your mom's coolers, or do they belong to someone else?"

Patsy considered a moment, shaking her curls playfully. "They're Mommy's!" she replied in a sing-song voice. "They're Mommy's—they used to be Uncle's and Auntie's, but they don't want them anymore!"

Busted.

"She doesn't understand the situation!" Mandy Reynolds stated hurriedly. "It's only temporary, until they want them back."

"That may be true, Ms. Reynolds, but public sentiment will surely be against your maintaining that position. We cannot force you to make any decisions, but those coolers are now considered communal resources, and a failure to share them will undoubtedly create feelings of justified animosity among your fellow residents."

Megan Bradley glared exultingly at her defeated nemesis and marched back to her seat. Reynolds sat down, fuming. Several snickers rippled through a crowd desperate for any source of amusement.

Barlette addressed the gathering. "We must be able to rely on each other in such times as these, and a desire to circumvent the plan only fosters a spirit of distrust in our community. We still have several minutes if any more cases needed to be brought forward."

A few hands went up.

"One more thing. Time constraints leave us no time for rebuttals. Speaking opportunities will be limited to the individual bringing the complaint."

Several more hands.

Barlette selected a young woman wearing yoga pants.

Smart. Gonna get sweaty anyway.

"Hi, I'm Jill Hodges, and I've got a few remarks to make on behalf of my husband, who couldn't be here tonight. Our next-door neighbors, the Holdens, have a large freezer in their garage which my husband noticed is still up and running. I guess they've got it powered somehow. Anyway, we don't believe this resource was reported in the general survey, and it seems like a waste since so many people right now have no means of storing food."

"Thank you, Ms. Hodges," Barlette said pleasantly. "Mr. or Mrs. Holden—whoever is present tonight—could you please come forward so we can all put a name to a face?"

A rather flustered-looking young man approached.

"Mr. Holden, do you understand the charges Ms. Hodges has brought?"

"Charges!" Holden snorted. "Sounds like a trial! Yes, I understand, and the fact of the matter is—"

"And do you realize the position in which you've put the community by not sharing your valuable resource?"

"Sharing my own damn freezer! It's mine, for Pete's sake, and I need space for more food items arriving soon. Jill, tell your nosy husband to mind his own damn business! I'll bet he doesn't give a crap about the community and is just mad about my not giving him freezer space for those fish he caught a few months back. As if I need a freezer full of smelly fish! And that's not all, either! He even expected—"

"Mr. Holden, I'm afraid you've forgotten the ground rules. I did not bring you up here to argue with Ms. Hodges but rather to acknowledge your understanding of the concerns she has raised. This ensures public accountability. As to disputing the charge, you are free to do that separately, in private communication with the Board."

Rob Holden turned red. "This is preposterous! Her husband's too much of a wimp to confront me directly, but she can question my integrity in front of everyone, and I'm not even allowed to respond? My wife and I supported the plan from the start while others were still bickering about it. Our records are clean! In fact, I was even going to report the Hodges for failing to—"

"Mr. Holden," Barlette interjected, "now is not the time. If additional support for the case is needed, I'm sure it will come to light. For now—"

"It sure will!" shouted another resident, now standing in the audience.

Football Man.

"I can support Jill's accusation. I know her husband, and he's got that big-ass freezer just sittin' there. Mostly empty, too! All my food went bad, and here he is, witholdin' resources!"

"You're a damn liar!" Holden retorted. "You just have old grievances, same as Hodges. Except with you it wasn't fish, it was some nasty wild pig or something. A whole animal! Why don't you—"

"You little weasel!" shrieked Rogers in a surprisingly high voice. "You're the liar!" He paused to catch his breath, giving Barlette an opportunity to regain control.

"Mr. Rogers, thank you for your comments. Mr. Holden, as I've already stated—"

"I ain't finished!" Rogers panted. "I've saved the best for last! This cheater knows more about the power outage than he cares to admit. He could get us out of this mess if he wanted to!"

"What's that supposed to mean?" growled Holden.

"Exactly what I said!" Rogers shot back. "'Freezer Boy' here is some sort of bigwig at the power company. He's responsible for the pain we're all goin' through!"

"You're a damn liar!" Holden yelled. "I've got nothing to do with it! Just because I work for a utility provider doesn't mean—"

"He admits it!" Rogers croaked exultingly. The crowd began to buzz with voices.

"No, I don't admit anything! I've done nothing, and—"

Barlette interjected once again. "Mr. Holden, please take a seat while we sort this out."

"I'm not going anywhere until I've had my say!" Holden shouted back. "And what are you all looking at?" he yelled at the audience. "You can all go to hell for all I care!"

An overheated, stressed, and impatient crowd immediately gave vent to days' worth of pent-up frustration. Rob

Holden found himself the subject of jeers, yells, and exclamations of general contempt hurled from a room full of normal people in a very abnormal state of agitation. Few remained sitting. Fisher and Barlette eventually abandoned their futile appeals for silence and retreated to the safety of the table onstage.

Watching the proceedings with grim amusement, the man suddenly heard a faint and unfamiliar voice. He strained to listen.

"This is quite unreasonable, everyone!" a thin, wheedling voice cried.

The mayor.

"Please, please, everyone—calm down, please!"

Sounds like a fat seal. Looks like one, too.

The exhausted crowd gradually quieted at the sight of the corpulent mayor. Residents regained their seats, only to observe yet another unexpected event.

The figure of Ryan Jackson materialized onstage.

What's he doing?

Before any of the surprised Board members could react, Jackson walked directly to the table and took the microphone from the mayor's hand before gently but firmly pushing the perspiring dignitary down into his chair. He beamed a wide grin at the expectant audience.

"Hey, everyone! Glad to see all of you here! If I may just—"

"Now hold on a second!"

"Yes?" Ryan replied calmly. "Is there a problem, Mr. Barlette?"

"Well, yes, there's a problem," Barlette responded hesitantly. "I don't know who you are, but it's not your place to be up here. We're running this meeting."

"Or it's running you," Ryan responded with another grin. Several audience members laughed. "I'm here to help fix this mess. Ryan Jackson's my name."

"I don't see—"

"I assure you, Mr. Barlette, you'll want to hear what I have to say."

Barlette glanced at Fisher, who met his glance and shrugged.

"Great, glad that's settled. I assure you, I speak only out of necessity. I believe that—"

"Now, hang on!" squawked a somewhat revived mayor.

"Mr. Rawlings, I guarantee that you and certain Board members will be most interested in what I have to say. Most interested, indeed!"

The audience members leaned forward expectantly in their chairs.

The mayor looked confused and frightened.

"I don't understand! It's not my fault! I—"

"I didn't say it was your fault. Whatever *it* is." Ryan looked up and down the table. "Any further questions before I begin?"

Everyone onstage looked uncomfortable but remained silent.

"Friends, our community is struggling. We're faced with an unprecedented and unexpected event. We've been given the plan, but we've still got a problem no one has addressed, one which threatens to tear us apart from within."

The crowd listened with undivided attention.

"Now, I'm a straight talker."

And a long one.

"No fancy language from me—you've had enough of that this week. I tell it how it is. And when I see injustice, especially injustice coming from the highest levels—the very people, in fact, in charge of helping the little man—I feel the need to act. It comes naturally to me. I believe in the goodness of the human spirit. That most folks want the best for others and will do good by those around them. Sometimes, however, bad apples attain positions of power which they use to stifle the common man. That's us—you and me. Normal people. The ones who actually *do* the work. Who care for each other and our families. Who live normal lives. We don't need much, and we don't ask much. We just ask for a fair shot."

A few murmurs of agreement.

"And, right now, I tell you, we are *not* being given a fair shot!"

More approbation, louder than before.

"Some people use power to hurt others. And these people are here among us and even lead us. But before I get to that, just think about this past week. Think about what's been done, the meetings we've had, the resolutions passed, the requirements imposed. A lot has happened. And lest anyone get the wrong impression I disagree with the plan, I believe our leadership team has done a commendable job in implementing such an endeavor."

Fisher's strained expression relaxed into a modest smile.

"But back to my point. Think about what you've seen over the last week, but, more importantly, think about what you *haven't* seen. Noticed anything . . . missing?"

Confused silence.

I'd like to be missing—somewhere else entirely until this is all over.

"Let me be more specific. Have you noticed anything or *anyone* missing?"

More silence.

"Okay, let's break this down in simple terms. We've been having daily meetings, right?"

The crowd nodded.

"And these meetings are for a select few or for everyone?"

"Everyone!" several voices called out.

"Right. And attendance at these meetings is optional or mandatory?"

"Mandatory!"

Freaking mandatory.

"Correct. Mandatory for everyone. Or *is* it?" Ryan lowered his voice mysteriously. "Just think. This is a large community. Has everyone been at the meetings? *Everyone?*"

Silence.

Probably not . . .

"No, they haven't! This raises several questions. First, does it matter? Yes, it does. Regulations must be applied equally to foster a spirit of cooperation and trust. Second, how do I know? By observation—*detailed* observation. By tracking attendance each meeting using the community roster posted online. I've observed several notable trends, including the complete absence of certain individuals all week long.

"Finally, who's the guilty party? The answer, naturally enough, is the people with the most power and influence.

"'So what?' you might ask. First, remember I'm not here to criticize the plan but rather the hypocrisy exhibited by some in positions of power. I don't know about you, but when I see the rich and mighty living by a separate set of rules, I get suspicious. Not of the system but of the people running it. Even the best systems can produce flawed results with the wrong people in charge. And that's what's happened here."

Ryan paused and withdrew a folded piece of paper from his back pocket.

"Here's a list of the individuals continually absent without leave. I don't want to name names, but, almost without exception, the names on this list belong to people directly connected to the Board. All the bigwigs covering for each other, it seems. Rules for thee, not for me. Attendance is mandatory! Mandatory, unless you're, say . . . Reginald Bates, for example, and then the rules don't apply to you."

Lawrence Fisher glanced up sharply but remained quiet.

"And Mr. Bates is only one example. Some residents have even been exempted from the plan itself and its pesky obligations to share resources with us plebs. And who might these people be?"

Ryan paused dramatically and waved the paper over his head.

"The same people on this list! The same people! With the important addition of the fine folks sitting up here behind me, who, I'm sorry to say, have exempted themselves from the very plan they forced on us!"

Angry exclamations filled the hall as Fisher sprang to his feet.

"Friends, I regret that our generosity in allowing this individual to speak has resulted in scurrilous and baseless accusations being directed at the very people who are trying hardest to help our community. The Board has worked tirelessly to make the plan a success and, in doing so, to bring a measure of security back to our community in these difficult times. Even our beloved mayor, who has many pressing concerns, is here tonight to address his devoted constituents."

Beloved? Devoted?

"And with what result? An unprecedented level of antagonism and ungrateful churlishness on the part of this dissident?! Unprecedented, truly anomalous behavior!"

Enough with the big words.

Fisher sighed. "However, we, as leaders, must take criticism in stride. It's part of the job, I suppose. We are continually subject to flawed critiques from those to whom leadership is merely a vague concept. Such is life. I hope, sir,"—Fisher turned toward Ryan—"you learn to appreciate the sacrifice we leaders make every single day on behalf of the very people who criticize our efforts."

Fisher sat down. Ryan smiled magnanimously.

"Mr. Chairman, I believe I speak for all of us when I commend the plan in its entirety. And, yes, implementing the

Plan required significant effort, and, for that, we are grateful. That is not the issue at stake, however. Nor does effort on your part exempt you from having to follow your own rules. Are you denying the allegations I laid forth?"

"All of us have acted with the interests of the community uppermost in our minds."

"That wasn't my question. What we want to know is if you and your cronies here are following your own rules."

"Well, we haven't been participating in the plan per se . . ."

You bastard!

A wave of indignant exclamations met Fisher as he hurriedly resumed.

". . . but that's only because we determined separately that our time and resources would best be spent in other areas. We've actually sacrificed more than those who've simply contributed physical resources. Ours is an intellectual and mental endeavor of a very strenuous nature! We are not receiving any special privileges."

"That's interesting. Very interesting, indeed." Ryan paused and eyed Fisher slyly while slowly pulling another piece of paper from his pocket. The chairman watched him nervously.

"Do you know what this is?" Ryan waved the paper before Fisher's face.

"A piece of paper?"

"Very astute, Mr. Chairman. This piece of paper reports the utility usage for our community over the last week. No need to ask how I obtained it—I've got my sources. Anyway, this report is very simple. It gives exact figures for the amount of electricity and water used by our little paradise here. While the numbers show a significant decrease from previous weeks, they still indicate some usage during the outage. How is this possible? As it turns out, several homes within this community have been up and running for days now."

The crowd listened with rapt attention.

"When the power went out, it went out for everyone. Same for the water. Miraculously, however, a few of our residents were back up and running a short time later. And can anyone venture a guess as to whom the utilities gods had smiled upon?"

"That's enough!" Fisher exclaimed. "We've let you have your say. You have no position of authority whatsoever, and—"

"Please, Mr. Chairman, I haven't finished."

"I don't care! I'm in charge here, and I'm tired of you acting like I've done something wrong!"

"Guilty conscience speaking, Mr. Chairman?"

"Not at all! I merely—"

"Perhaps I can change that. Of the names I've been able to obtain, yours stands out above the rest. You currently have both electricity and running water in your home. Nice little system! Utilities go down; implement a plan to address the problem; exempt yourself from the responsibilities of said plan; use your powerful connections to ensure your own comfort; then come back here and lecture us all on community spirit and cooperation. A nice little racket. A racket, I say!" Ryan proclaimed, raising his fist dramatically. "We've had enough! We're drawing the line here! *A chairman who oppresses the people we don't need!*"

The crowd erupted in raucous support for Ryan and open condemnation of the hapless Fisher. The man joined in enthusiastically. Unified shouts of "*Out! Out! Out!*" soon rang through the hall. Several minutes passed before Ryan could finally speak.

"Glad we're all settled down now. I didn't expect such a strong reaction to my comments! I just saw a problem and decided to fix it. No desire to be up here in the first place. Now that we've all calmed down, we have some issues to address. Everyone still on board?"

The crowd nodded in unison.

"Great! So, first issue. It's clear at this point that the current leadership structure of this community is not conducive to its general well-being."

"No, *no*!"

"The question remains: what must be done? Do we all consider the Plan beneficial?"

"Yes, *yes*!"

"Good, I thought so. The system is not to blame." Ryan cast a disdainful glance at the sullen group of Board members sitting at the table. "Mr. Fisher?"

The chairman glanced up quickly, like a hunted animal. "Yes?"

"I regret that you can no longer lead our community endeavor. I believe in second chances, but, for your own well-being and safety, I feel an obligation to separate you from our rightly-indignant community members who, as you have just seen, can be quite difficult to control. Due to this unfortunate reality, I'm afraid someone else is going to have to take charge."

"And that's the question I have for you," Ryan continued, addressing the crowd. "Who should lead us?"

The consensus was universal: they wanted Ryan Jackson.

Ryan, feigning surprise, shook his head modestly, but the calls grew louder. Within a minute, a unified crowd chanting his name forced him to raise his hands in acquiescence.

"Friends, I don't know what to say. In my own plain way, I must express my appreciation for the trust you seem to place in me. I doubt I'm the right man for the job, but I serve where I am called."

The gathered residents clapped enthusiastically.

"Now, I will need your help. I expect to rely on all of you, some especially so. With me at the helm and all of you at the oars, we can bring this ship safely into harbor. Until then, *onward*!"

More cheers.

"Then everything's settled . . . everything except the issue of compliance for these fine folks behind me. Now I'm a forgiving guy at heart, so I'm for overlooking the whole matter and moving forward. That sound like a good plan?"

It did not sound like a good plan to the gathered residents, who loudly voiced their displeasure toward the Board. Ryan considered their response.

"Mr. Fisher, I find myself facing unforeseen circumstances. When I took it upon myself—out of a sense of obligation, mind you—to hold you accountable this evening, I had no idea I would end up assuming your leadership role."

A slight hint of a sneer briefly crossed Fisher's face.

He knows you planned it.

"And now I find myself forced to determine the best means of restitution. This is not about revenge, and I'm sure my neighbors are merely looking out for the interests of the community when they seek this redress of grievances. I don't believe in penalties myself. It's time to move forward, not back. I realize you didn't act alone and shouldn't take the fall for everyone who betrayed the public trust. We'll eventually get around to confronting everyone on my list of shame, even guys like Bates who seem . . ."

Fisher's expression instantly changed from a look of glum apathy to one of intense concentration. Ryan failed to notice.

". . . rather untouchable. In fact, if you can provide us with insider information to aid our quest for community justice, perhaps we can forget about any penalties whatsoever. How's that sound?"

Ryan now glanced at Fisher, whose cunning expression startled him. The chairman spoke.

"So, Mr. Jackson, you want some information, do you? Well, I'd be happy to give it to you."

A pause. Ryan waited, but found no explanation forthcoming.

"Uh . . . great, glad to hear it! Seems like some of this unpleasantness could have been avoided if—"

"I have one condition, that being a full and complete exculpation of any wrongdoing or involvement in this little affair. That's all."

"*All?*" Ryan responded incredulously. "Why, that's the crux of the whole matter! You did wrong—everyone knows it. I can't provide expectoration even if I wanted to."

"Maybe drink more water," Fisher replied tartly. "You want information, you play by my rules. I guarantee it'll be worth it. You think you know everything that's going on around here, but you don't. Not even close. I, however, *do* know."

Fisher leaned back in his chair and settled himself comfortably.

"I understand the workings of this community, Mr. Jackson. I understand who really makes the decisions. You think I direct events or perhaps the mayor or one of these individuals beside me. But you're wrong. I wish I had significant power, but I don't. It's for this reason that I must insist on a full repeal of any accusations brought against me over the last week. I've simply been following the orders of those who pull the strings. These people are powerful, and they get what they want. It's the way of the world. The group is quite small—just a few people, in fact. And I'll let you in on their dirty little secrets."

Fisher leaned back even further in his chair and cracked his knuckles. Ryan stood pondering the chairman's offer, clearly intrigued but not anxious to show signs of interest. He turned to the crowd.

"Well, what do we think? As a community, do we accept or decline Mr. Fisher's offer?"

Silence.

I don't know . . . he's a sneaky one, that Fisher . . .

Ryan realized he would have to take the lead. "I think we're all on board with you, Mr. Fisher. Sounds like a fair trade, but, mind you, it must be valuable information."

"Oh, it's valuable, all right! So, it's a deal?"

"Yup," Ryan said, once more scanning the crowd and receiving no pushback.

Fisher leaned forward.

"Bottom line, this neighborhood is really controlled by a few rich and powerful people."

Like you?

"I could describe how they sabotaged my efforts to shape this community for the better; believe me, many words would fail to fully reveal the extent of their control and my inability to combat their influence. Many words might be necessary at some point, but right now one is sufficient. One word, Mr. Jackson—you want to hear it?"

Ryan waited expectantly.

"One word—*Bates*."

Ryan started and eyed Fisher suspiciously but with the look of satisfaction one derives from having a long-held belief confirmed.

Fisher grinned.

"Well, Mr. Jackson?"

"Bates?" Ryan feigned ignorance. "Let's see . . . oh yes, he's one of the names on my list. So let me get this straight—you're saying he's at the bottom of this?"

"I'm saying he ultimately controls everything that goes on around here. He makes his own rules. Perhaps you've noticed his absence over the last week? That's pretty much how he operates. And I happen to know his mega-mansion is operating just like normal—no power outage, no water issues, nothing."

"So he has clout when it comes to resources," Ryan pressed, "but are you saying he controls everything? In other words, was this outage an accident of which he took advantage, or was it planned from the beginning for some purpose?"

"That's something you'll have to ask him directly. Maybe have another meeting and require his attendance? It should only take a couple hours."

"Hell no!" a voice in the crowd called out. "All we do is have meetings! He won't come, anyway."

"How else do you plan on confronting him? It's not like you show up at his house or anything!"

"That's exactly what we should do!" announced the new speaker, an ordinary-looking man standing in the crowd. "If he won't come to us, we'll go to him!"

The crowd responded enthusiastically. Fisher affected a look of astonishment.

"Go to his house?! Surely just a few of you to discuss matters privately! No large or unruly group making demands . . ."

"Right again!" chirped the ordinary-looking man. "You're full of good ideas, Mr. Chairman! We'll go as a group!"

The crowd agreed.

Ryan, having gauged popular sentiment, now raised his hand for quiet.

"Okay, everyone, I see we've all decided on a course of action, one which will require some time to be put into effect . . ."

"I say, act now!" the ordinary-looking man called out.

". . . tomorrow, if all goes well. It's almost Friday, thank goodness! It's been a long week, but, hopefully, we can get some answers before the weekend. How about we meet here tomorrow afternoon and then go see our friend Bates?"

The proposal met with exuberant support.

"One other thing," Fisher cautioned. "The key to success lies in keeping things under wraps. Bates must not know about it beforehand. He's sneaky and cunning."

Again, like you.

"It must be kept secret. I myself will help lead, as I've got a few things to settle with . . . that is . . . I want to prove my dedication to our community by striking at the heart of the problem."

"And I'll help!" exclaimed the ordinary-looking man. "I can shout real loud!"

Obviously.

"And I'll do the actual leading," Ryan stated, trying to regain control. "For the sake of the community, of course. It's time to bring this situation to an end! Tomorrow marks a week since the outage began, and what has actually been achieved in that time? Nothing! In fact, things have only gotten worse!"

The crowd expressed indignant agreement.

"And who's suffered the most? We have! Not the nameless, faceless powers that be. But now those powers have a face and a name, and that name is Bates! He's accountable for everything—for toilets that don't flush, for spoiled food . . ."

Ryan was now yelling to be heard over the sound of the raucously supportive crowd.

". . . for hot and sleepless nights, for crying kids, for all our problems! Now is the time to act! Not only for ourselves but also for our families and those who rely on us for their well-being. Not as individuals but as a unified community. And anyone who sabotages that community has to go!"

Ryan's voice was drowned out completely.

Friday—Reprise

DAYBREAK. HALLELUJAH. LIGHT, NATURAL LIGHT. HAZY LIGHT. Or maybe that's just my eyes. So tired. Everything's blurry. What time is it? Have to take a sick day. Might not have what the kids have, but exhaustion ain't much better. What do they have? Maybe food poisoning? That's what she thinks. Said it was my fault, that I'd done something. Me? Yes, you. How so? Maybe you left food out too long. Nope, we've been eating takeout, and that stuff lasts forever. Maybe they ate something you didn't cook thoroughly. What did I cook? Hotdogs. Seriously? They got food poisoning from some franks? I nuked those things, and they're precooked anyway. That's what I should've said. Why didn't I? Too tired, perhaps. What time was that? Maybe one or two? Seems like a month ago. What day is it now? Must be Friday. Funny. This all started last Friday. And all because of Bates. At least that's what Fisher says . . . and now, Ryan. Don't generally trust Fisher, but I think he's right this time. And Ryan had a theory about Bates before any of the meetings even started. Guess he's got some foresight. Or maybe one of his crazy theories is bound to be correct eventually. Of all his theories, I want this one to be true. That

113

Bates character just rubs me the wrong way. Self-entitled jackass, up there in his chateau. Was he up all night, covered in vomit and sweat? No. Is his wife—whichever one he's on now—yelling at him like mine is? Maybe. Probably, actually. Even the elite have problems. And he's got a big one now, because we've had enough. I've had enough. Can't take another night of this. Don't even know how I'm getting through today. Asleep, that's how. Sound asleep. Starting right now before the kids wake up.

The man tiptoed down the hall to avoid his wife as she cleaned a large stain off the living room carpet. He reached the bedroom without observation and quietly closed the door, collapsing onto the bed without even removing his slippers.

His cell phone suddenly rang. He ignored it. Three times he ignored it until he heard the text tone and began fumbling in his bathrobe pocket with his eyes still closed. He opened his eyes and stared at the screen, trying to make the fuzzy blur focus into something legible.

"CALL ME NOW." The man groaned and called his boss.

❦

Ryan had been busy, very busy. Yesterday's meeting had gone well, but Fisher had emerged intact. The guy had the resilience of a cockroach. Still, it might work out better in the end. Ryan had never liked Bates, nor did he like his friends and neighbors always poking fun at his theories. Now, he'd do the laughing. He'd told 'em beforehand. Some of them, at least, including his next-door neighbor, the one whose help Ryan now needed.

He glanced at his watch and dialed his friend's number.

"*What*?!"

"Woah, calm down, chief!" Ryan laughed. "Why so touchy?"

"Ryan? Thought it was someone from work. Why they can't just leave me alone on my off day is beyond me."

"Not at work? That's perfect! I'll need your help later, but if you're in the neighborhood—literally!—maybe you could lend me a hand now?"

A long pause.

"Not really in the mood, Ryan . . . honestly, I'm barely even awake right now. Running on empty. Last night—the kids sick, no rest . . ."

"Look, I'm sorry you've got family problems, but we've all got issues right now. I'm pretty exhausted myself. But I need your help."

"Why me?"

"Because I can rely on you."

Ah, the benefits of being dependable.

"So whaddya say? You willing to lend a hand?"

"With what?"

"The Bates matter—I need to make sure today goes well. And you're just the man to lead this initiative."

"Aren't you leading?"

"Yes, at least visibly. I'll be the face of the movement, but I need a logistical organizer, a behind-the-scenes man to work out the details."

"What details? We show up at the hall and then walk or drive over to Bates's house. Simple enough."

"Yeah, but I'm talking about the psychological element."

"The *what*? Explain please, doctor."

"It's like this. These residents are a volatile and unpredictable bunch. They're volatile because they're mad and unpredictable because they're just regular suburban people with no experience handling this sort of situation. One minute, they're raging mad, and the next, they're playing with their kids and minding their own business."

"Isn't that a good thing?"

"Sure, but, for our purposes, we need consistency. Consistent outrage."

"Outrage?"

"Yes. Not too much—just enough to let Bates know he can't bargain his way out of this one."

"You want people mad is what you're saying."

"They're already mad; they just haven't realized it yet. That's where you come in."

"Ryan, I'm so tired, man . . ."

"Just hang on for today," Ryan urged. "Make it to the weekend, and hopefully by then, everything will be resolved."

"You really think Bates can fix things just like that?"

"I don't think it matters one way or the other. Bates is an ass who's had it coming for a long time, and taking him down should help us get Fisher and the others as well. What'd you think of my little performance yesterday? Pretty good, huh?"

"Performance?"

"You know, the whole deal about the Board not following their own rules and getting special privileges."

"Isn't that true, though?"

"Sure, at least the part about the plan. The rest was pretty ludicrous, but the crowd went for it."

"Wait, so Fisher and the others don't have power in their homes?"

"No, how could they?"

"But . . . the report! And why wouldn't they just deny it?"

"The report doesn't exist—that was a bluff . . . and a damn good one, too! They aren't denying it because doing so would involve admitting to living in a fancy hotel for the last week using community funds. As soon as I discovered that juicy tidbit, I knew we could use it to our advantage."

"Our?"

"Yes, we're all in this together. Especially you, since I need you to help me."

"But couldn't you find someone else who might be better?"

"Nope, you're the man for it. I know I can rely on you to keep the crowd motivated."

"I just don't feel it—all I feel is extreme exhaustion."

"That's it? You're not the least bit mad about this whole situation yourself?"

"Of course I'm mad—I'm freaking *pissed*! This whole week . . . the more I think about it, the more pissed off I get!"

"Then keep thinking about it," Ryan said. "I want you mad, especially since you can control your emotions better than most. How 'bout it? Just for today, then I'll leave you alone. Deal?"

The man heaved a sigh. "Okay, deal."

"Sweet. By the way, everything okay at home with the wife?"

"Yeah, everything's okay. Just a lot of squabbling, but I'll make it up to her when this is over. Maybe take her out for dinner or something."

"Or cook for her," Ryan suggested.

"As long as it's not franks."

"What?"

"Nothing. We'll be okay. But after today, I'm done."

"Nothing after today, I promise," Ryan replied cheerily. "Just give me everything today, and make sure you're in the right mindset. I need outrage and aggression—better get yourself amped up."

"No need, Ryan. I'm plenty pissed off already. Just give me the game plan."

⁊

The man scanned the noisy gathering and started as someone tapped him on the shoulder.

"Ryan! Didn't see you. It's about time you got here—we need to get going."

"My thoughts exactly. Just had to check some intel I got. Did you know"—Ryan lowered his voice—"that Bracken and his family left this morning?"

"Left? They're not in the neighborhood?"

"They're probably not even in the state by now."

"Meaning?"

"They left this morning—packed that big SUV of theirs and left. Headed for a relative's place out of state, apparently. I'm surprised you didn't even notice."

"Ryan, this morning I wouldn't have noticed an elephant sitting in Bracken's yard."

Ryan grinned. "It's not a huge deal, except it'll be more difficult to use his resources for the community like we planned. Still, Bracken was more Fisher's concern. Have you seen the honorable chairman yet, by the way?"

The man shook his head. "You're the first leader to show up, as you can see by the empty table up there."

Ryan chuckled. "They're probably all friends of Bates, anyway. I just hope none of them warned him of our plans. I still don't trust Fisher, but what he said about secrecy seems valid. We can't let Bates know we're showing up."

"He must know by now," the man replied. "I mean, look—the whole neighborhood's here."

He was right. The building was virtually bursting at the seams. Amid the din of confused noises, he saw Fisher walking confidently toward them. He nudged Ryan, who nodded smugly. "Let's get this party started."

⁓

The man trudged down the street, trying to keep his eyes open. Drowsiness overwhelmed him, and the sun bouncing off the pavement hurt his eyes. It was bright. And hot.

Damn hot. Unreasonably hot.

The chaotic hubbub of the surrounding crowd only made his raging headache worse.

Geez, they make a racket! Maybe wait to start chanting until we arrive at the house? Still got a mile to go. Why'd we even walk? Need some water. C'mon, stay focused.

❦

They had arrived. The man snapped out of his self-pitying reverie when he found himself standing on Bates's massive front lawn. Ryan, megaphone in hand, stood in front, leading the crowd in a chant. The man felt too tired to join in as he made his way through the sweaty throng. Glancing toward the house, he suddenly noticed Bates emerging onto a second-floor balcony. Dressed in white trousers and a dazzling pink golf polo, the neighborhood mogul held a drink in one hand and a cigar in the other.

Bates regarded the crowd with a mixture of suave aloofness and confused uncertainty. He finally began waving the hand with the cigar in an effort to silence the crowd. After several fruitless attempts, Ryan came to his aid.

"Attention, please!" The call was repeated several times before it took effect.

"Thank you," Ryan said, still speaking into the megaphone. "In fairness to Mr. Bates, I feel it's only right to inform him of our reasons for being here—obvious though they may be—and to allow him to respond. Mr. Bates," Ryan called, looking up toward the balcony, "are you aware of the cause of this gathering?"

Bates, vacillating between an inclination to ignore the rabble entirely and a desire to exert his authority, decided on the latter course of action. He placed his drink on the balcony railing.

"I don't know what's going on here, but I need everyone off the grass. You're destroying the work of my landscapers."

Not a great start, dude—we've got no A/C or water and you're moaning about the damn grass?

The crowd agreed and made their frustration clear, forcing Bates to change tack.

"Never mind," he called out with forced carelessness. "They'll fix it. I would appreciate, however, someone filling me in here?"

I'll fill you in, all right. Right on the noggin.

"I don't know what's going on. Is something wrong?"

Ryan hushed the indignant crowd. "As a matter of fact, Mr. Bates, something is very wrong. Even though you have not graced our recent meetings with your presence, I'm sure you're aware of the crisis that has affected our community for a week now. No water, no power. The whole community. Almost. Your neighbors, kindhearted though they may be, have reached a point of understandable vexation. They want answers, and you're capable of providing those answers. So we're here to get them."

A short round of applause burst from the crowd.

"Hold on a minute," Bates retorted. "Start at the beginning. What's your name again?"

"Jackson, the duly appointed representative for these fine folks behind me."

"Oh yeah—Riley, isn't it? You're the talkative fella that kept asking me questions earlier this week."

"Yes, I did talk to you earlier this week, and, in fact, about the same topic we're here to address. You might call it a bit of intuition on my part. I anticipated this entire situation because I have observed how you operate and the tricks you pull."

"What is this?" Bates erupted, contemptuously flicking his cigar over the railing. "You come here with your friends and start talking trash without any explanation? Out with it, man!"

Before Ryan could respond, Fisher materialized beside him and eagerly seized the megaphone.

"You know what's going on, Bates! You know full well! These people are here because they know the shenanigans you've been up to! I told them! They came after me, but you and I both know you're the one making decisions around here. And now they're mad, Bates! Aren't you? Aren't *you*?"

The crowd responded with enthusiastic cheers.

Bates glared at Fisher. "Ah, it's you, Larry! I should've known you'd be at the bottom of whatever's going on. I'm just surprised you got so many people to go along with you."

"Whatever's going on?" Fisher countered. "You know full well what's going on! You're living the high life in your palace while we lesser folks suffer."

We?

"Everyone knows you control the utilities!"

"That's what this is about?" Bates asked. He snorted. "Go to hell, Fisher! You told everyone I control the water and electricity in their homes? You're an ass! I've got no control over any of that. If I've got power, it's because I paid lots of hard-earned moolah for a backup system. Maybe you should do the same—you could use your own cash or even appropriate community funds like the last time . . ."

"Don't deflect, Bates!" Fisher hurriedly cut in. "The people want straight answers!"

Ryan Jackson snatched the megaphone back from the chairman and addressed Bates.

"Don't focus on Fisher, Bates. It's not about him. I'm leading this effort on behalf of your neighbors here. They're pissed, Bates. You don't give a damn about anyone or even care about their suffering!"

"And what the hell am I supposed to do about—"

"You know full well, Bates!" Ryan yelled, turning to the crowd. "Don't we?!"

The crowd began yelling again and pushed forward until those in front stood almost directly underneath the balcony, with Ryan now perched on a small garden rock feature.

"It's all your fault, Bates!" he shouted. "Deny all you want!"

"Hell yes, I'm denying it! I've got nothing to do with it, and you still haven't explained how I could possibly—"

A loud smack. Bates now stood, clearly shocked, his soaked pink polo turning purple. The crowd roared with laughter.

"Take that!" the ordinary-looking man shouted. "Consider it a favor! A water balloon beats no air conditioning any day!"

Bates's face turned the same color as his shirt. "Why, you little—damn you!" he bellowed. "Get your ass off my yard before I rip you apart!"

"Make me!" came the shrill reply. The crowd cheered. Cries of "*Out*! *Out*! *Out*!" reverberated through the hot afternoon stillness.

"I'll call the police!"

"You do that!" Ryan yelled into his megaphone. "Call the police? What a coward!"

"*Police*! *Police*! *Police*!"

"Call the police—we don't care! We'll be back tomorrow, and the day after that, and the one after that . . . every day, Bates! You'll get no rest until we've received justice!"

"*No rest*! *No rest*! *No rest*!"

Bates made an almighty effort to control his simmering outrage. The magnate found himself in a novel situation, one in which his wealth and influence for once had no mitigating effect. Torn between contempt for those standing below him and a desire to win their admiration and envy, he contemplated his remaining options. He could call the authorities, but asking for help would hurt both his pride and his standing in the community. Bates, normally impervious to social antipathy, began to understand the implications of the entire neighborhood using him as a scapegoat of sorts. How to get them off his back without degrading himself?

Suddenly, an idea hit him. Deny, then reaccuse. Who? Fisher. *Definitely* Fisher. The little cheat was undoubtedly behind all this. No, that was too risky—the chairman had the crowd on his side. Who then? Someone nobody would defend. Someone recognizable, but without connections. Someone slightly mysterious. Someone . . . *that's* it!

Bates shook himself and tried to focus. Raising one hand, he waited for Ryan to hush the crowd before speaking.

"I see I'm up against a determined bunch here," he began. "That's good—I'm pretty bullheaded myself. I like to see people attack a problem. Fact is, though, you've attacked the wrong problem or, in this case, person. I realize my great life and cool toys make it hard for most of you to relate to my position, but I'm an understanding guy at heart. I also admire passion and dedication. I support what you're doing, but you need to direct your complaints elsewhere."

"He's lying! Stop deflecting! We're on to you, Bates!" The crowd's agitation increased.

"And not just anywhere," Bates continued. "Those grievances must be addressed to one specific person. And I know who."

"Lies!" cried Fisher. "Don't listen to him! I had nothing to do with it—"

Bates cut him off. "It's not you, Larry, though you certainly deserve it! It's not you. It's someone few people know anything about, besides me. He's the most mysterious character in this entire community."

The crowd listened, their curiosity piqued.

"He rarely shows himself. He talks strange and acts even stranger. Nobody knows his real name, only his title. I refer, of course, to the professor."

The . . .?

The bemused audience gave no reply, but their silence encouraged Bates.

"Let me break it down for you. The professor is a recluse whom many of you have never seen. He doesn't attend our meetings."

"Neither do you!" a voice shouted. Bates waved his hand dismissively and continued.

"He never shows up for anything, really. No one knows where he comes from or what he does. I mean, he's called the professor, so maybe he is one, but how do we know? I don't think he is! Think about it. How does a professor live in a neighborhood like this? I know what it takes to live like a king, and it's more than an academic salary, I assure you. Speaking of dough, the professor is a hardcore miser who pinches pennies at your expense. He even refused to pay his community garden fund fee! I mean, what the hell?! The guy's got millions, and he makes you pay for neighborhood upkeep! Trust me, I've seen that geezer do stuff that would make Ebenezer Scrooge indignant!"

"Where's all this leading, Bates?" Ryan asked suspiciously. "Why does any of this matter?"

"It matters," Bates thundered, slamming his fist down on the railing, "because this same miser owns everything around here! He controls it! You think I'm powerful because I own a few houses? That dude owns this whole freaking neighborhood! And it doesn't end there. Riley here thinks I somehow control the power company. Well, I don't, as I've said. But guess who does own it? That's right—the professor!"

The crowd listened intently. Encouraged, Bates continued crafting his juicy narrative.

"Yup, he holds the purse strings. And what's terrifying"—Bates lowered his voice, forcing the crowd to strain to hear—"is that he controls your air conditioning, your lights, your refrigerator. And your water—yup, he's got that, too. All under his sovereign control. Bet you didn't know that, did you? Now here's where it gets good. My high-level connections tell me utility companies are hemorrhaging cash right now and are looking for new ways to cut costs. The professor, faced with the same dilemma, has decided in all his stingy shrewdness to screw us all! He cut your power to save himself some cash!"

A subdued murmur of indignation swept through the crowd.

Is this legit? First Fisher, then Bates, now the professor . . . whom to trust? That sort of thing does happen . . . seemed nice when I met him . . . you never really know, though . . .

"That miserly snake has deprived you of the basic necessities of life in order to fix his balance sheets! That's all it comes down to—his ledgers over your lives!"

"How do we know this is true?" a voice called out.

"It isn't true!" Fisher interjected. "He's just deflecting blame!"

"Speak for yourself, Fisher!" Bates roared, shaking his fist at the chairman. "This all started with you! Why, I bet you're even involved with the professor yourself! He never recruited you for his schemes? Never randomly showed up at your house on some pretense, acting all friendly for no reason? Maybe talking about his stupid books?"

Wait.

"That's what he does!" Bates continued. "Tries to gain access to people, feel them out."

"I'm completely blameless in this matter," Fisher protested, sensing the crowd had moved in support of Bates. "I'm just having trouble believing some eccentric recluse is behind all this. I'm open to persuasion, but I need more evidence."

Guess it's true, then. Bates clearly knows how the professor operates. What a fool I am—completely taken in! Thought he was just some kooky old man. Wonder what he wanted from me?

Before Bates could respond, the man stepped toward Ryan and took the megaphone with a wink at his neighbor.

I've got a plan.

Ryan, eyeing him quizzically, stepped down onto the grass as the man assumed his perch and turned to face the crowd.

"I've got proof, folks. Bates is correct—the professor is up to no good. Just a week or so ago, he preyed upon me in the exact manner Bates described. I didn't realize it at the time, but he took advantage of an act of kindness on my part to further his own designs."

Bates listened gleefully.

"What do we think?" the man continued, addressing the crowd. "Should we take this up with the professor or all disperse to those sweatboxes previously referred to affectionately as our homes? I believe now is the time for action! We've had a week of talk—let's do something for once!"

Several shouts of support.

"He's right!" Bates called out. "That old bastard has played you all for fools! He's exploiting your empathy, your kindness. He knows you're all good, decent people who wouldn't dare hold any suspicions for fear of causing offense. You're too good, in fact! Well, sometimes when being good don't work, you gotta be a little bad!"

The crowd cheered, now thoroughly persuaded.

"What do we do?" a voice called out over the din. "How do we be bad?"

Bates grinned. "It doesn't take much. You've gotta face the issue head-on and confront him directly."

"How? We never even see him!"

"You never see him because he doesn't come to you. So, if he doesn't come to you, what's the other option?"

"We go to him!"

"Bingo!" Bates yelled. The crowd cheered again.

"Let's go!" the man called out over the megaphone. "Who's with me?"

Bates smirked as he watched the exuberant throng flood back into the street. Retrieving his drink, he went inside.

❧

The crowd made its way onward, slowly approaching the most remote part of the neighborhood.

Walked a lot today. Probably tired . . . lot quieter now.

The man watched the hot and thirsty residents trudge along, their enthusiasm waning. *Have to get them pumped up again.*

"Almost there, folks!"

Ryan sidled up to the man and spoke to him in an undertone. "What did you have in mind if the old geezer's not home? He rarely is, apparently. Or maybe he just hides in there and doesn't come out."

"Uh, I'm not sure. I was hoping you'd think of something."

"Me? But you led us all here."

"It's your show, Ryan—I'm just helping out. I think I've done pretty well, actually. Going after Bates was never going to work. Dude's too powerful. Besides, I believe what he said about the professor, who seems like a more manageable target anyway."

"I don't know," Ryan replied glumly. "I don't like Bates—I'll admit that straight out. I still think he's involved somehow. Sucks to see him get out of it so easy." Ryan kicked a small pebble down the street.

"Maybe so, but we aren't going to get anywhere with him. I'd think you'd be grateful for my efforts! Put aside your personal animus toward Bates and focus on the new task at hand. I've got a bunch of hot, tired people to deal with, and the last thing I need is for you to start griping. You came to me for help, remember?"

"Okay, okay," Ryan responded soothingly. "I'm just a little flustered, that's all." He glanced around. "Say, I should really come to this part of the neighborhood more often. It's so secluded and quiet, or it would be without all the people."

"Yeah, it's nice."

A few minutes later, the man found himself standing on the professor's neatly manicured front lawn, the crowd waiting behind him in the road. He took stock of the situation. The house, set far back from the street, looked deserted as usual. No station wagon sat parked on the long driveway. Everything was quiet.

Need some noise.

"What's the matter?" the man called over the megaphone. "We just gonna stand around, or what? Let's make some noise and show him we mean business!"

The crowd began chanting. "*Come on out, Pro-fess-or!
Come on out, Pro-fess-or!*"

The house remained perfectly silent with no sign of life.

The man, certain the noise could be heard from inside, strolled up the lawn, stopping in front of the house and some distance from the crowd. He raised his megaphone.

"Professor, we'd like a word, sir. Please come on out."

"Come on out! Come on out!"

No response.

"Professor, we're not leaving until you come out!"

Unless he's not home. Then what?

The crowd grew quiet. The man advanced to the front door and knocked loudly. Nothing happened. He knocked again.

Come on!

Suddenly, the door opened just a crack. As the man tried to peer into the gloomy darkness within, a female voice spoke.

"Who is it?"

The crowd, unable to hear the resident's voice, strained to catch the man's reply.

"Um, ma'am . . . is the professor at home?"

"Why you asking?"

"We'd like to talk to him about something."

"Why the people here?"

The man thought he detected a tremor of fear in the faint voice.

"Oh, don't worry about them; they don't mean anything. I just want to talk to the professor. Are you his housekeeper?"

"He not here. Not here right now. Not back until—"

"Not back until when? Later tonight?"

No reply.

"Okay, thanks anyway . . . don't want to bother you any-more . . . talk some other time." The man slowly backed away.

This place is weird. Wish I could at least see who's talking.

"Okay, bye!" The door closed.

Creepy.

The man turned around and tried to think as he walked toward the crowd.

Sounds like he'll be home later. That's something to go on, at least.

He reached the curb and stopped, scanning the expectant throng before raising his bullhorn.

"Here's the situation, folks—there's been a slight change of plans. I've been informed the professor is not home but will be later this evening."

The crowd groaned.

"I know, I know," the man responded hastily. "I realize we've been trekking around all afternoon, and we're hot and tired. It's been a long day . . . a long week. We all need some rest. But how can we rest? We go home, and we're faced with stifling heat and no utilities. We've got to act now. Just hang in there a little longer! Let's get this done before the weekend."

"What do we do?" a voice questioned.

"We still have to talk to the professor," the man replied.

"Let's go stand in the shade and wait until he comes back. That way, we can't miss him."

"True, we wouldn't miss him, but we'd face other problems. First, we'd be on private property. Second, this is the professor's home turf, and he might be less willing to compromise. No, we need to confront him where we have the upper hand. We choose the battleground, make him play by our rules. The best place to do that? The neighborhood entrance!"

The assembly remained silent.

"We can't miss him! He'll be caught by surprise, and we'll make him listen to what we've got to say. How's that sound?"

A few fatigued residents muttered their support.

"That's all the energy you can muster? Come on, everyone—think of your family members back home, all sweaty and miserable, because one old miser thinks he can pull a fast one on us. You may not care, but I sure do, and I'll act on my own if necessary!"

The man began marching down the street.

Come on . . . please follow!

The crowd, ashamed of their hesitation, now let out a resolute cheer and fell in behind.

Yes, that's it.

"There we go, folks! Glad we're all in this together! One more final push."

ॐ

Surely, she meant later today. And not too late, hopefully. Damn it. Getting dark, and everyone's tired and hungry. Saw several sneak off. Where's Ryan?

The man turned, looking for his friend, whom he spotted sitting on the curb across the street.

"Ryan!" The man jogged over to his neighbor. "What's up, man?"

Ryan sighed. "I'm tired. Tired and ready for some grub."

"Come on, don't you start! You're the real leader here! I'm only here as a favor to you, after you dragged me into this when I was the one needing rest."

Ryan hopped up from the curb, stung by his friend's rebuke.

"I know, man—I'm better now. Felt kind of overheated, actually. At least it's cooler now the sun's gone down."

"If you're feeling better, I need your help."

"With what?"

"Advice. I need to know what to do if the professor doesn't show up."

"What do you mean?"

"I mean if we're all out here waiting for who knows how long and he never shows up. What do we do then?"

"You mean you don't even know if he's coming?" Ryan asked incredulously.

"No, I don't know! Not for sure, at least. How could I? I thought his housekeeper, or whoever it was, meant he was on his way home, but now I'm not so sure."

"That's not good."

"Yeah, no kidding! But what else was I supposed to do? Tell the crowd to go home, sorry for making you tramp around in the heat all day for no reason? I had to do something! If you had a better idea, why didn't you mention it?"

"Okay, okay. It wasn't meant as a criticism. You took me by surprise, that's all. We just have to figure out what to do. If too many people leave, we'll have problems—how many do you think we need to confront the professor?"

"Just a few, but that's not the point. We need the entire community involved. They need to have skin in the game so we're all in this together. Confronting the professor here will ensure nobody will back out."

Ryan nodded as he glanced around uneasily. "Makes sense to me. But we still haven't figured out what to do if he doesn't show. You don't think they'd turn on us if things don't work out?"

"No, but they'd take us for fools and we'd lose whatever authority we have. Technically speaking, we don't have any actual authority, but I think the people consider us their leaders now."

"Yeah, and I don't relish the thought of all my neighbors hating my guts. We've got to avoid trouble."

"Yup." The man surveyed the crowd, then stopped. "Hold on!"

"What's up?" asked Ryan, quickly looking around.

The crowd seemed agitated. Groups standing on the grass on both sides of the road looked toward the entrance, with others standing in the street to get a better view. As the noise grew, the man turned toward the entrance, not daring to raise his hopes too high.

The straight driveway off the main road lit up as headlights pierced the gathering darkness.

It's a station wagon! Thank goodness.

"Okay, everyone, here he comes!"

The crowd instantly sprang to life. A confused yet enthusiastic babble of shouts and cheers broke out as the throng flooded into the now obstructed street.

After passing the welcoming flowerbeds and landscape features, the approaching vehicle suddenly stopped a few dozen yards away.

He sees us.

After a moment's pause, the car began to crawl forward until it reached the assembly, the crowd giving way and closing around both sides of the vehicle as it rolled slowly onward before again coming to a halt. As the crowd watched in silent expectation, the car door slowly opened and the professor cautiously emerged.

"What is happening here? Everything okay?"

The crowd remained silent, uncertain how to address the smiling elderly gentleman whom some were now seeing for the first time. This was not the mysterious villain they had imagined.

"Is there problem?"

The man shook himself, realizing his focus on the professor's sought-after arrival marked the extent of his planning.

Great, now what?

He looked to Ryan for help but found his neighbor standing behind him, carefully avoiding eye contact by staring intently at the professor.

Damn it, Ryan! I know you see me.

The crowd remained motionless, the long silence growing unbearably awkward.

The man cleared his throat. "Uh . . . Mr. Professor, sir."

Mr. Professor?! What a dumb . . .

"Yes? What is it?"

"Uh, I suppose you're wondering why we're all gathered here like this?"

"Yes, this is very strange. Everything okay, no?"

"Yes, well, uh . . . no, not exactly. I mean, we're fine . . . sort of, but you . . ."

"Yes?"

Come on, you coward—spit it out! He's the bad guy here.

"We're fine, sir, but . . . you aren't, exactly. Not fine, I mean."

"How I not fine?"

Stop smiling! Makes it harder.

"Sir, as I'm sure you're aware, the utilities for this entire neighborhood have been out for a week now. Mostly. Some exceptions exist—you currently have power, correct?"

"Yes, I have power. I—"

"Exactly. You do, but we don't. Everyone here has no power, no water, nothing."

"Why they not do what I do? I show them how to—"

"Show them how to . . . what, exactly? Screw over an entire neighborhood?" The man spoke aggressively, eager to make up for his initial timidity.

"I not understand." The smile melted from the professor's face.

"Don't you now? Well, we do, sir."

The professor looked around uneasily. "I still not understand."

"I think you do. These fine people have waited all evening for some answers."

"Answers to what?"

"Answers to why we've been living in the Dark Ages for a week. We want answers, and the answers so far all point to some sketchy stuff going on."

"Sketchy?"

"Yes, sketchy. It means suspicious or nefarious."

"Oh, I know nefarious."

Of course you do.

"What is nefarious here?"

"The cause of the power outage is what's sketchy . . . *nefarious*. Turns out, it's not some unforeseen accident or unavoidable necessity but rather predetermined malice. But you know this already."

"No, I know nothing. I still confused why we need discuss this here in road. Why not have meeting?"

"We've had meetings, Professor," the man replied with rising anger, "but you weren't there! Not a single time! So, if you won't deign to come to us, we'll come to you, as you see."

The professor, visibly taken aback by the man's vehemence, tried to respond. "I not know we have meetings! Nobody tell me."

"Ever heard of the internet?" the man scoffed.

Maybe not, actually.

"Anyway, we're getting sidetracked. Fact is, there's a problem, and we're here to deal with it."

"But what problem?"

The man spoke slowly through clenched jaw. "Let me spell everything out really simply. We've got no power, right?"

"Yes."

"Right. For a week now, no power. No explanation, no known cause. We've had meetings with lots of talking and heated discussions. Blame cast all over the place. But, in the end, the conclusion we reached is that you're at the bottom of all this."

The professor viewed him quizzically, hands clasped before him. He looked almost comical in his vest and bowtie.

And who wears a derby, anyway?

"Me? You think I cause problem? That why you all here?"

Eureka!

"Yes, Professor. That's what we think and *know*."

"But why come here? Can we talk different time? I late for dinner—housekeeper angry when I not punctilious about schedule."

Damn, he likes that word.

"Your housekeeper can wait—we've already talked to her."

The professor started.

"Yup, we went to your house earlier but got nowhere. So we came here."

"But what you think I do?"

"We know you have control over the situation here and have put your own personal enrichment ahead of the welfare of this community."

"I not control anything—"

"Furthermore, we're here to put an end to this."

"But I not control anything! I only live here."

"You don't run or own the electric company?"

The professor shook his head, clearly baffled.

"You don't control who has electricity and running water in this neighborhood?"

The professor shook his head again, this time smiling incredulously. "No. How I do that?"

"So how do you still have utilities while the rest of us don't?"

"I make preparations," the professor replied eagerly, anxious to elaborate. The man hastily interrupted.

"Never mind—it doesn't matter."

He tried to think. He could see residents casting questioning glances at each other as they found themselves standing in the middle of the road on a Friday night, listening to someone they barely knew talk to an old man they definitely didn't know. They were tired and confused, and they barely even remembered why they were there or what the professor had to do with anything. Something had to be done . . . and right away.

The man turned, searching for Ryan. His neighbor had vanished.

What the—?! Where'd he go? Damn sneak . . . got me involved and leaves as soon as things go sideways. Now I'll get the blame! Got to make this work.

The sound of a car door closing cut short his distressing train of thought.

Not so fast, buster!

The man ran up to the car and spoke through the open window.

"Hold on, Professor. Where do you think you're going?"

"Home."

"You're not leaving, Professor. We won't let you leave until we've worked things out. Will we?"

The man turned to the crowd. They remained silent, uncertain.

Damn it, people!

"I leaving," the professor said firmly, the car lurching forward.

"No, stop!" The man planted himself in front of the car, leaning on the hood. "Stop! We haven't finished talking!"

The wagon halted, engine idling.

"Hold on, Professor! You trying to run me over?"

"Why you stand in the road?"

"We want to talk to you!"

"We? You are only one talking this whole time."

"I speak for everyone here. Isn't that right, folks?"

The man turned and surveyed the crowd but failed to receive any reply. Many looked visibly uncomfortable and averted their eyes as the professor, now standing hunched over the doorframe, cast a troubled gaze in their direction.

Got to do something!

"I'm ashamed of you folks. Really! *Ashamed*! We're so close to our goal, and now all you want to do is . . . well, nothing. Just stand there with your hands in your pockets. What have we worked all day for—all week for!—only to give up with the goal in sight?"

A voice piped up. "What is the goal?"

"The goal is—"

Damn it . . .

He tried again. "The goal is to fix this issue we've been having for a week now."

"How's this going to fix it? We've been walking and shouting all day, and now we're standing in the road and I don't even remember why I'm here!"

A general murmur of assent ran through the crowd.

Damn it!!

"We're here because the professor is responsible for the past week of misery!"

"I know nothing about it—"

"He's responsible, and you all know it—you've been with me all day!"

"That's right, all day!" sang out another voice. "All freaking day, and all it's come to is yelling at some geezer who looks more like my kooky uncle than a villain."

Several residents laughed.

"You think it's funny?" the man sputtered. "Everyone out here having a jolly old time while your families roast in sweltering homes! Is that what you want?"

"As long as it keeps the wife quiet—can't whine and nag when you've got heatstroke!"

The quip provoked universal merriment.

The man paused, fuming.

No appreciation. Dragged into this, worked my ass off, and they think it's all a joke! I'll be one, for sure. Hey, remember the time that one resident—I forget his name—thought the old professor was somehow cutting off our electricity? And how he brought us all out to protest in the street? Wasn't that a laugh?

"Happy, are we? That's nice, *real* nice. I'm so glad for all of you. You see, I'm not happy. I'm outraged! I'm outraged on behalf of those in our community who are suffering and who rely on us for help. And what are we doing? Ignoring them! Giving up the fight, all because we're tired and unwilling to act now that our goal's in sight. It's shameful!"

The man's boiling anger, manifested as righteous indignation, seemed to have some effect.

"We want things fixed as well!" a resident called out. "We just don't think targeting the professor is the way to do it."

"This is right—I not do anything!"

"You shut up! Everyone seemed pretty convinced of his guilt just a short while ago! You all chicken out?" the man sneered.

"We need proof!" The crowd nodded in agreement.

"Proof? The proof's right in front of your face! An entire neighborhood suffering while this jackass has everything his heart desires. Worse still, he clearly hasn't participated in the plan or even attended our meetings."

"I not know—"

"Shut up, dammit! He thinks he's too good for us! Doesn't give a damn about the community or anyone but himself! I've had it! I've had it with him, and I've had it with a bunch of sissies who chicken out the moment they're really needed! Pathetic!"

"I help with others if you like. Let me alone—I not cause problem!"

"Shut up! Shut up, you old fool!"

The man bounded forward and slammed the car door shut as his adversary retreated several steps backward. The crowd, shamed into action, moved forward slightly.

"Yeah, shut up, old man!"

"Think you're better than us, huh?"

The professor stood blinking nervously in the deepening blackness, his initial bewilderment now replaced by outright fear. Realizing his attempts at rational discussion were proving futile, he mustered the courage required for a more direct approach.

"I not better than anyone, but I not subservient either. I not understand this whole affair, but right now I going home. I make report of this if you keep me here."

As the professor took a few steps toward his station wagon, the man stepped between him and the running vehicle.

"Report us?" he jeered. "Report to whom? The whole neighborhood's here!"

The professor hesitated.

"Just realized you're all alone, eh? Can't talk your way out of this one! You're alone and, judging by the look on your face, very afraid." The man grinned.

The professor tried to get past the man, but he only succeeded in prompting his inquisitor to reach inside and turn off the puttering engine.

"Give me my keys! Why you take them?"

The man raised the keys tauntingly before tossing them into the throng. Everyone laughed. The professor made a feeble rush but found himself rebuffed by a raucous crowd now surging forward, whooping with delight at the tragically comic image of the panting academic beating a quick retreat.

"Think you can run away from us on those scrawny legs of yours, eh, Professor?" The man and the crowd behind him kept advancing, forcing the professor to clumsily stumble backward toward the main road.

Now we've got him!

The professor halted, out of both space and breath, and glanced first at the crowd spread in the street before him and then over his shoulder at the passing cars. With no options left, he summoned his remaining resolve and stepped toward the man. Their eyes locked.

"Give me my keys," he said quietly, holding out a trembling hand.

"We're keeping your keys, old man."

No response. The hand remained outstretched as the crowd grew tensely quiet.

"Lower your hand!" the man growled, trying to sound intimidating.

Nothing.

The man stepped forward, now close enough to smell the antique mustiness of the professor's clothes.

"Move back!"

"You approach me. I did not move."

"Move back, and drop your hand!" The man swatted the professor's hand aside, only to see it outstretched once more.

"Give me my keys. You have no right to take them."

"I'm warning you—I will act! You think I won't? What do you think I am?"

"A gull."

"A what?"

"A dupe."

The man started. He stared at the owl eyes through the shiny spectacles. The professor was right. He *was* a dupe! His anger completely vanished as he stood contemplating his own naivete and the ridiculous spectacle he certainly presented at that moment, totally at the mercy of some old man who engendered more sympathy than anger. The crowd, despite its aggression, mainly sought entertainment, and while their hostile posturing might scare the professor, the man knew they'd stop short of actual violence. Even the man's own bluster had been just that—impotent frustration channeled into attempts to scare his foe and motivate the crowd. But now they'd direct their laughs at him, a mere puppet manipulated by forces beyond his control.

I'm a dupe, all right, and they know it.

Suddenly, an idea struck him. A crazy, insane idea. An idea so crazy, it wasn't crazy. The man studied the Face as it loomed gigantic before him, its blinking orbs mockingly brilliant in the enveloping darkness. He breathed deeply.

It'll only work if I'm calm. If everyone knows I'm in complete control of myself and my emotions. That I did it purposefully, knowing the consequences. Because that's not something a mere pawn would ever do.

His contemplations came to an abrupt end as a brilliant surge of light left him momentarily stunned. The entire entrance driveway instantly came to life, streetlamps lighting the pavement and attractive electric lanterns at ground level casting a warm glow over the parallel sidewalk. The crowd, equally dazed, stood blinking confusedly and shaking their heads before turning silently to each other in disbelief.

The man, his eyes now accustomed to the dazzling light, collected his thoughts and returned his gaze to the Face, now glowing with a mixture of visible relief and gratitude. The idea returned, stronger now. *Much* stronger.

Stepping slowly and deliberately up to the professor, he struck.

The man felt a buzzing sensation in his hand but also a complete calm which pervaded his entire body. The shocked crowd stood motionless, their mouths agape, terrified of the man's composed manner which frightened them more than the actions of a raving madman.

"Why you hit me?" The words came out thickly.

The man calmly regarded his quarry before striking again, sending the professor staggering backward. With a terrified shriek, the academic turned to flee but found himself facing the main road. The crowd, horrible in its motionless indecision, surrounded him on all other sides. With terrifying coolness, the man grabbed the professor, shook him until his teeth rattled, and flung him to the ground.

"Stop! Rostopchin! *Stop!*"

The man pursued his sordid task, his fists rising and falling with the precision and impassivity of a clock chiming the hours as the Face melted into a bloody, gurgling mess. Silence reigned, the only sound the dull thud of hard bone on soft flesh.

☙

A pedestrian strolling past the glittering neighborhood encounters a troubling vision. A crowd of people, all rooted to the spot in frozen horror, surround several objects on the grass beside the road. One figure stands out, the methodical wiping of stained hands on a small handkerchief the only movement exhibited in the entire gathering. At the foot of the fastidious individual lies a large bundle. This bundle, when viewed intently, reveals limbs twisted and splayed in a manner unnatural to humans. For human, it is . . . or had once been . . . though now it was merely a tattered mass of bloody flesh.

Shocked and repulsed by this scene, the passerby wrests his gaze from the victim to the nearby objects, a soiled felt hat and a large, impressive sign illuminated by discreet spotlights. The sign appears brand new, leftover dirt from the recent installation still visible around its base. A few trays of flowers, not yet planted, lie scattered nearby. Visible from the main road, the sign stands like a mute sentinel mere yards away from the grotesque tragedy.

The lettering is clear and bold; the message, unassuming:

WELCOME TO TRANQUILITY BIGHT
A NURTURING, PEACEFUL COMMUNITY

Acknowledgments

A massive thanks to my fantastic editor Gail and book designer Melinda! Y'all turned a good idea into a great reality, correcting my errors and providing guidance while preserving the less orthodox elements of my writing, perhaps to my future shame.

To my family, who were blindsided by this book and are hopefully not too embarrassed by it, thank you for your support and encouragement over the years. Love each of you!

About the Author

An avid reader, Bahr Burr's interest in creating the written word continues to grow as required college writing assignments fade into the merciful oblivion of forgotten memories. Bahr explores themes of human nature and moral agency in his reading and writing journey. His favorite author is Dostoevsky.

A native Texan, Bahr enjoys eating meat and watching rugby, ideally simultaneously.

Leave a Review

Did this book impact you in some way? Cause you to shed tears of wonder and awe at the magisterial genius of the concepts and philosophies expressed herein? Prompt a fit of dignified spluttering as you choked on your latte in a fit of righteous indignation at the supremely offensive drivel you somehow couldn't force yourself to stop reading? I'd like to hear your thoughts! Submit an honest, articulate review on the platform of your choice, and I'll probably read it. Probably. It will be cathartic for you, and I'll get the joy of knowing I prevented your using those ten minutes of your life for something actually productive.

Or you can subscribe to my Substack and yell at me in the comments while engaging in your masochistic desire to read random essays that fail to meet your cultured standards.

Find me at bahrburr.substack.com.

—Bahr

www.ingramcontent.com/pod-product-compliance
Lightning Source LLC
Chambersburg PA
CBHW050856180626
46814CB00007B/2766